Crafted with LOVE

Also by Leanne Malloy

Sewing Up Some Love

Crafted WITH LOVE

Book #2 in the Indiana Romance Series

LEANNE MALLOY

Copyright © 2019 Leanne Malloy

This is a work of fiction. All of the characters, names, incidents, organizations, and dialogue in this novel are either the products of the author's imagination or are used fictitiously.

All rights reserved. No part of this book may be used or reproduced by any means, graphic, electronic, or mechanical, including photocopying, recording, taping or by any information storage retrieval system without the written permission of the author except in the case of brief quotations embodied in critical articles and reviews.

WestBow Press books may be ordered through booksellers or by contacting:

WestBow Press
A Division of Thomas Nelson & Zondervan
1663 Liberty Drive
Bloomington, IN 47403
www.westbowpress.com
1 (866) 928-1240

Because of the dynamic nature of the Internet, any web addresses or links contained in this book may have changed since publication and may no longer be valid. The views expressed in this work are solely those of the author and do not necessarily reflect the views of the publisher, and the publisher hereby disclaims any responsibility for them.

Any people depicted in stock imagery provided by Getty Images are models, and such images are being used for illustrative purposes only.
Certain stock imagery © Getty Images.

Scripture taken from the Holy Bible, NEW INTERNATIONAL VERSION®. Copyright © 1973, 1978, 1984 by Biblica, Inc. All rights reserved worldwide. Used by permission. NEW INTERNATIONAL VERSION® and NIV® are registered trademarks of Biblica, Inc. Use of either trademark for the offering of goods or services requires the prior written consent of Biblica US, Inc.

ISBN: 978-1-9736-6817-6 (sc)
ISBN: 978-1-9736-6819-0 (hc)
ISBN: 978-1-9736-6818-3 (e)

Library of Congress Control Number: 2019909160

Print information available on the last page.

WestBow Press rev. date: 8/2/2019

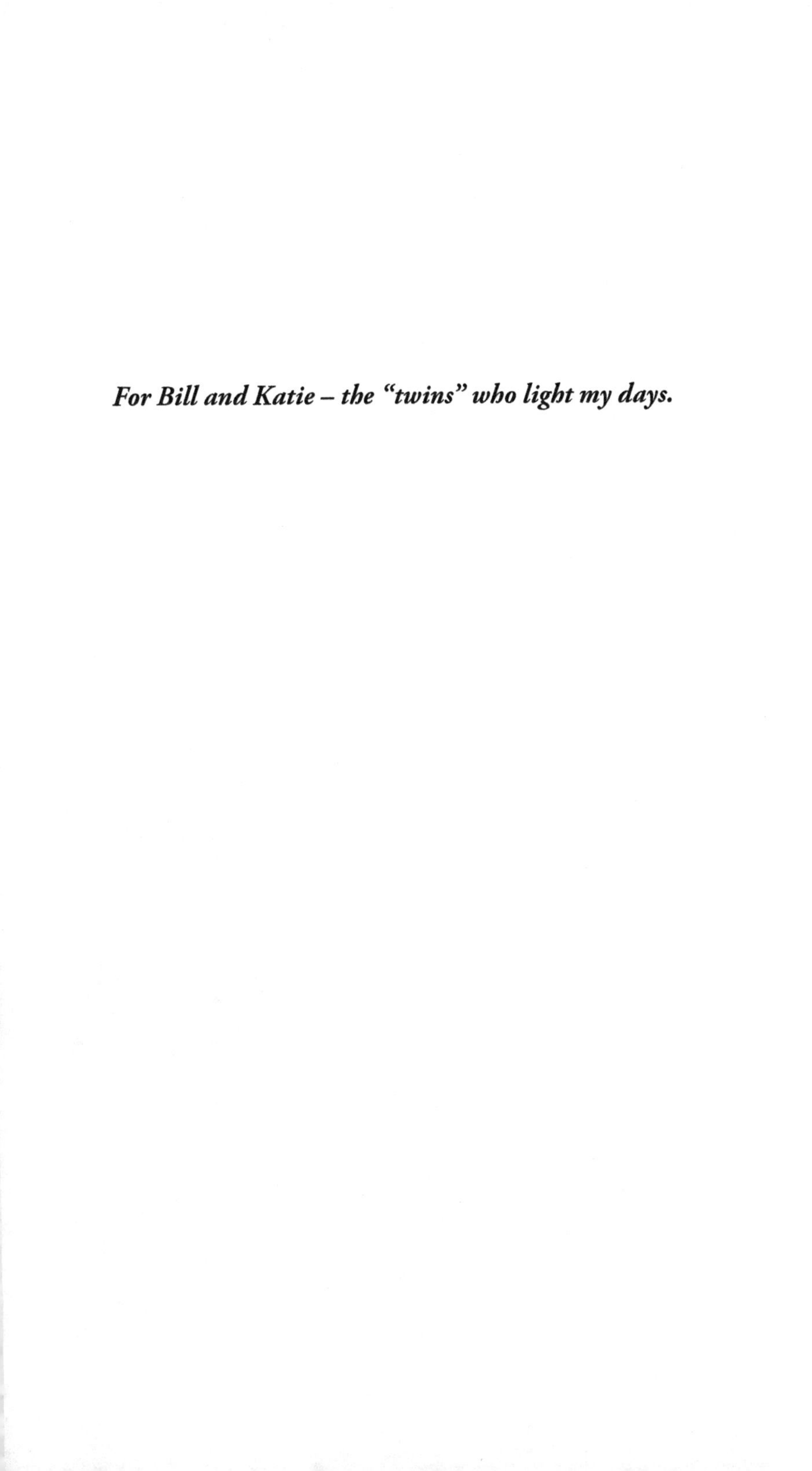

For Bill and Katie – the "twins" who light my days.

Contents

Prologue

Well, that's done, Kristen thought as she blew out an exaggerated sigh. She was glad she'd been honest with Lauren about the breakup with Rob. The senior counselor's opinion meant a lot. Rob's love of black clothing, which he'd disguised as his input to help Kristen relate to her adolescent clients, had led to Lauren's questions about Kristen's new fashion sense. Lauren had been kind and accepting, not dismissive, when Kristen revealed the reason for her black ensembles.

That's probably why she's such a good counselor, Kristen thought. *"Be kind, but not stupid," Lauren had said. I need to achieve more of that balance. I'm plenty kind, but I was pretty stupid with Rob.*

Kristen knew her own counseling skills were improving rapidly, though in mental health there was always much to learn. Unfortunately, Ricky, her new supervisor, relished picking apart Kristen's case notes each week during their weekly supervision session. Her previous boss, Dr. Cheaney, had actually praised Kristen's growing insights with clients. Ricky seemed to see nothing of merit in Kristen's work, despite Ricky referring the most challenging cases to her. Kristen also noted Ricky wasn't seeing any new clients herself, which meant the other counselors had even heavier caseloads.

Kristen's optimism returned as she left the mental health center. She loved her job and counted herself lucky to have graduated from an excellent counseling psychology program. She passed her licensure exam with a great score and accumulated training hours quickly. Returning to Gordon, Indiana, after grad school was another stroke of luck. The mental health center had been hiring, and Dr. Cheaney took a risk with Kristen. Life was good.

Except in the romance department. Kristen had broken up with

Rob soon after his admission that he liked her in black clothes. While her anger at her old high school boyfriend had dissipated, Kristen was still irritated with herself. How could she have fallen for such a manipulative message? Rob was into Goth *and* his new secretary, not Kristen.

So, I've learned a tough lesson. Just because you've known a guy for years, there's no guarantee you ***really*** *know him. It's easy to overlook the obvious when you're too comfortable.*

As she opened the door to her apartment, Bernie bounded into her, landing his furry paws on her shoulders. His Golden-Doodle enthusiasm, along with his typical "best day ever" approach to life, helped Kristen put thoughts of Rob out of her mind. After sufficient hugs and praise for her "handsome boy," she noticed the missed call and message on her cell. Her mother's voice sounded pleased.

"Honey, Dad's appointment with Dr. Schneider went great! No more radiation is needed for now. He's cleared Dad for our trip to Grand Cayman. Isn't that terrific?"

Kristen noticed two worrisome things in her mother's message. Dad was done with radiation *for now.* And her mom's enthusiasm was directed more to the upcoming vacation than her dad's health status. Typical. She forced herself to return her mother's call, more for her father's sake than anything else.

"Great news, Mom," Kristen said. "How's Dad feeling? Still tired? Is his GI distress better?"

"So much emphasis on the negative, honey," Kaye Anderson chided. "Why can't you focus on the fact that Dad and I get to go to the beach? Dad's stomach is fine if he watches what he eats."

"Wonderful, Mom. I'm happy you and Dad get to go on your vacation. You both deserve a break."

"Too bad you and Rob can't come with us as we'd planned. I'm still fuzzy about why you ended it with him after all these years. He's a good guy."

Unwilling to replay the no-win argument again, Kristen

responded, "He is a good guy, Mom. But for someone else, not me. Hey, I've got another call. Talk to you soon."

Kristen hated lying about the nonexistent call, but she was tired of trying to explain the changes in Rob to her mother. Or maybe she'd changed, not him. Whatever the case, after she'd earned her doctoral degree and been hired at the mental health center, Rob began to remark that she probably didn't want to be with a mere electrician anymore. Nothing Kristen said would lessen Rob's sense of insecurity. In fact, she'd noticed his growing comments about the new receptionist at the union office. Just before their breakup, he'd commented on what a great listener she was as opposed to Kristen, who he claimed only wanted to talk about work politics and mental health funding.

Probably true. I'm too focused on work most days, but I think I'm getting better. And I sure wouldn't sink to lying about Rob's choice of clothing if I felt uncertain about our relationship! He actually made more money than I did, but I never cared about that.

Bernie chose that moment to remind Kristen, (via a loud bark while standing next to his food bowl), that dinner was running late. Kristen laughed and said, "Bernie, I need a man like you. No games, no pretense. Just straightforward communication about what you need, with lots of love in return."

Chapter One

Two Years Later

Kristen's honey-colored hair was curlier than usual as she ambled to the starting line for Gordon's annual Fourth of July 5K. Nothing like Indiana humidity to cause her hair to spiral even further out of control. Dressed for comfort, not style, she stretched and twisted to loosen up before the race. Her faded top and baggy shorts belied the strong runner inside. No need for trendy sports bras or skin-tight leggings. Kristen believed in the value of a fast heartbeat and a cleansing sweat, both served well by her comfortable clothing.

"Looks like there's a better crowd than last year," her friend Annie said. "We're all probably running in anticipation of the hot dogs and potato salad we'll gorge on later. I'm glad I didn't give my students a project prior to the holiday weekend. Summer courses are taxing enough. So there's no grading on my to-do list. My only task is to enjoy the holiday eats."

"It's a good crowd," Kristen agreed as she eyed the group, looking for people she knew. "But no hot dogs for me. Per Mom's request, her final Indiana dinner will be spare ribs with homemade barbecue sauce. She had me test four recipes before she approved the final winner, which has more garlic than you can imagine. She also said I have to simmer the ribs on the stovetop before they go on the grill for finishing. It's kind of funny, since she's never been much of a chef."

"I can't believe she's moving away - to Arizona, no less," Annie said. "What's your sister think about that? I'm sure she's wondering what kind of care your mom will require."

"You know Katie," Kristen said, tying her shoelaces tight. "She's a roll-with-the-punches gal. Mom's senior apartment is almost an hour from Katie's house, so she thinks that's a safe distance for healthy boundaries."

"Boundaries? Is that psych code for not driving Katie nuts?"

Kristen grimaced. "Yes, I was trying to be kind. To both Mom and Katie. Since Dad died, Mom's been floundering. She thinks Arizona will cure her grief, and she's sure the weather will help her arthritis. She might be right about the last point. Mom's a healthy sixty-something, so Katie thinks she'll adapt quickly. We tried to get her to wait six more months to move, but she insists on going now. Dad's only been gone since January, but there's no convincing Mom that a change of scenery won't lessen her pain."

Kristen remembered the agony of the phone call from her mother, describing her father's sudden death, despite his successful bout with cancer. Her only solace was that her beloved father hadn't suffered. The cardiac arrest had been quick and final.

"I see the hurt in your eyes, Kristen," Annie said. "How are you doing?"

"I'm okay," Kristen said, after a long pause and a silent gulp. "The hybrid course I launched in June keeps me distracted. Online teaching looks deceptively simple, but the prep before the course launches is huge. I've got a good batch of students, and they love the format. And I can't say I miss the mental health center much, after all the changes that occurred. Teaching, a little private caseload on the side, and my craft business suit me fine."

"To each her own," Annie quipped, taking a big swallow of water followed by a healthy burp. "'High-tech/high-touch' leaves me cold. Classroom teaching is my love, but even my nursing course is about to go online. I'll be physically present with the students during the clinical rotations, but that's it."

Annie's carefree attitude was like a balm to Kristen, especially after her father's death. Despite her outward presentation, Annie was an intelligent, caring nursing instructor, holding a nurse practitioner's credential. She demanded a lot from her students, and in response, they had one of the highest pass rates on the state licensure exam each year.

Teaching at the community college had been a salvation of sorts for Kristen, both in terms of work she loved and her friendship with Annie. Kristen's psychology students were challenging but fun. After her father's death Kristen plunged into work, beginning a side business in reclaimed crafts, along with her private practice. She knew her friend was staying busy to avoid her grief and loneliness, but so far it was working. Mostly.

Her weekly garage sale shopping had been in full gear since May, when Indiana weather turned warm. Kristen had an eye for inexpensive, well-worn pieces she could turn into designer items. Her current projects included stuffed teddy bears made from old quilts, grapevine wreaths with seasonal flowers, and holiday vests fashioned from discarded Christmas tree skirts. Lately she'd thought about transitioning from selling her wares at flea markets to an online store, which could increase her sales significantly.

The pre-race warning horn ended all conversation between the two women. Kristen and Annie were soon off, running at a comfortable pace. Annie's running style was faster than Kristen's, and in a few minutes, she was several yards ahead. Kristen had no desire to win her age group. *When did I turn thirty, anyway?* Nor was she focused on improving her previous race time. Running helped her think, despite the distraction of the cheering crowd and the volunteers offering water every few yards. And she needed to think.

The last several months had crawled by. She missed her father's tender counsel. Without his presence, her mother was impulsive and self-absorbed. Intellectually, Kristen knew her mother was dealing with normal denial and grief, but Kaye's behavior was still difficult for Kristen. If she had a client with similar issues, she'd counsel patience and tenderness. But since Kristen was hurting too, her patience with her mother sometimes failed her.

Beyond her grief, Kristen felt isolated and alone. Rob's recent marriage reminded her she was no nearer to her dream of having a husband and kids. Dating wasn't the problem.

Men on singles' sites sought her out regularly. Compatibility, on the other hand, was a challenge. Most of her dates fell into one of two categories: those wanting first-date sex and those needing a stepmom for their kids. Kristen's steady income made her all the more attractive to the men who "swiped right."

And what about that steady income? Kristen's teaching skill was reflected in the positive evaluations from her students. But similar to the fate of the now-closed mental health center, Gordon's community college faced possible staff reductions due to decreased enrollments. Kristen wasn't concerned about losing her job entirely, just about cuts in salary and benefits. She needed to bolster her income streams. Teaching, crafting, and seeing clients in the evenings made her busy, but not rich. Barely comfortable, in fact.

Finding a good rhythm to her stride, Kristen thought about her options. She could increase her caseload, but that would mean Bernie would be alone more than he was now. An online craft store could increase her sales, but she would add shipping, insurance, and a payment system to her task list. And she enjoyed selling her wares at festivals and flea markets. Being able to meet people from across the country appealed to her extraverted nature. Another possibility was teaching adjunct courses at the college branch in the next county. She wasn't sure, however, if the cost of gas and mileage would cover the meager adjunct rate.

Kristen's anxious reverie was interrupted by the sound of whimpering coming from behind a large bush in a deserted part of the course. She raged at the thought that someone must have abandoned a puppy. Such cowardice was beyond belief. Bernie had helped her through so much distress that she couldn't envision anyone treating a dog cruelly. She slowed and walked carefully to the rear of the scraggly, squat tree. No puppy was to be found. Instead, a small girl sat in the shade.

"Hey, sweetie, what's wrong?" Kristen asked.

The little girl, dressed in red leggings and a flowing, sleeveless, royal-blue top, sniffed and wiped her eyes with both fists. Since her hands had been on the dusty ground, her face was now covered with dirt.

"I lost my daddy," she said. "I was going to surprise him when he won his race, so I left Grandma. Where's the finish line?"

"Honey, we have quite a way to go before the finish. I think we need to get you back to Grandma, so she doesn't worry about you too much."

"I'm not allowed to go anywhere with strangers," the girl said, standing and stamping her foot while generating even more tears. A loud hiccup punctuated her declaration.

"Okay, I'll introduce myself. I'm Kristen Anderson. I've lived in Gordon almost my whole life. I'm a teacher. What's your name?"

"I'm Sophie. You know we're still strangers, right? Just because you say your name doesn't mean I know you. I don't think I should go with you."

Smart kid.

"Yes, we're strangers, Sophie. But I can tell you want to get back to your grandma, and I'd like to help you. How about if we walk together back to the starting gate? I won't hold your hand or touch you, and you can yell for help if you feel scared. There are lots of people around who would hear you."

Sophie pondered this plan for a few seconds. "That sounds okay. But my daddy says I have strong lungs, so I'll yell if I need to."

"Got it," Kristen said. She smiled at the little girl, so fierce and terrified at the same time. Kristen pointed and said, "See those red, white, and blue balloons down the road? That's where we need to go."

"I see the balloons. Grandma was standing close to them." After a moment of studying Kristen, Sophie said, "You can hold my hand if you want. I won't yell."

Kristen and Sophie walked hand-in-hand toward the balloons, being careful to avoid the runners as they passed. Sophie revealed she was ready to start first grade, lived in Indianapolis with her mother, and was visiting her grandparents for the holiday.

"Do your mommy and daddy visit Gordon often?" Kristen asked.

"My mommy and my step-daddy, Grant, don't come here much. My daddy lives here now. I miss him lots."

"I see," Kristen said. Poor kid. Sounded like a recent divorce had upended her world. Her desire to see her daddy "win his race" was especially poignant.

Lots of meaning behind that wish.

A sweaty man with dark hair and icy blue eyes bounded up, scooping Sophie into his arms. "Sophie, where have you been?" he asked, glaring at Kristen. "Who's this lady?"

"I wanted to see you win the race, Daddy," Sophie said. "My friend, Kristen, was bringing me back to the balloons."

An older couple followed the angry man, pausing to catch their breath. Sophie reached out for her grandmother and announced, "Daddy's too yucky to hold me."

Introductions were made. Kristen explained her discovery of Sophie behind the bush. Luke and Jane Sutliff, who appeared to be in their late sixties, were mortified at allowing Sophie wander away. Their son, introduced simply as Mike, remained suspicious.

Kristen studied the emotional man. He seemed so quick to suspect her motives. What kind of experience had led him to react like that to someone who'd rescued his little girl? Kristen's psychological training instantly developed several theories, most of them centering on his being a part of an ugly, unwanted divorce.

As she looked at Mike, she noted Sophie's resemblance to her father. Each had the same crystal-blue eyes and dark, almost black, hair. Sophie's hair was done in a high ponytail tied with ribbons to coordinate with her patriotic outfit. Mike's straight hair kept falling in his eyes, adding to his irritation. Kristen gave him credit for his running togs, though. Like hers, they were evidently chosen for utility and comfort, not style. His T-shirt was so bleached out the featured rock band's name couldn't be distinguished. She guessed the band was some throwback from the eighties. And despite his baggy attire, his broad shoulders and muscular frame were obvious.

"So, you heard Sophie crying?" he continued. "Weren't you focused on the race? On making good time? How do we know you're who you say you are?"

Annie jogged to them, unaware of the tense conversation she was interrupting.

"Where did you go, Kristen? I made it to the finish, but you weren't behind me as usual. Are you okay?"

"I'm fine, Annie. I'll explain later," Kristen answered. Mike looked like he was ready to call the police. What was that saying? *No good deed goes unpunished.*

"Well, hi there, Dr. Sutliff," Annie said. "I didn't recognize you at first. And I didn't know you were a runner."

"Hi, Annie," Mike said grudgingly. Looking at Kristen and Annie, he continued. "I'd better take my parents and Sophie to the car. They've had an upsetting day. Kristen, I appreciate all you did for Sophie. Sorry if I came off as ungrateful. Obviously, you helped my little girl find us at the cost of your race. We're all thankful. You were Sophie's Good Samaritan today."

"Happy to help," Kristen said. Looking at Sophie, she continued. "You gave your daddy and grandparents a scare. Maybe the next time you want to surprise your daddy, you'll check with another grown-up first."

"I will," Sophie said, tearing up again. "But now I have you for a friend in Gordon. So that's good, right?"

Kristen grinned while Mike looked annoyed. "You've got a smart one on your hands, Mike. And she's good at reframing negatives into positives. Good luck."

"Guess that's my problem, not yours," he said to Kristen. "But thanks again for all you did to help Sophie today."

Mike turned to walk to his parents' car but stopped again. He appeared to be ashamed of his rude comment.

"Wait, Kristen," he said. "I'm sorry, again. Seems like I apologize to you every other sentence, and we've only just met. Your comment about Sophie is right on target, but it reminded me of someone I'd rather forget."

Kristen studied him, debating whether to continue the conversation. She decided to be brief. "I see. I'm sorry, too, if I upset you by bringing back unhappy times."

Mike herded his parents and Sophie in the direction of the parking lot. Sophie waved at Kristen and shouted, "Thank you!"

"Well, there's a story or two here," Annie said. "You can feel free to tell me anytime. I didn't know you and Dr. Sutliff knew each other."

"We don't," Kristen said. "I found his little girl lost and hiding behind a bush. He practically accused me of abducting her!"

Kristen began to walk to her car. Suddenly, she circled around to face Annie. "Wait a second," she said, almost growling. "Was that the Dr. Sutliff from the hospital? I left him a message earlier this week, suggesting a new antidepressant assessment for one of his patients. I see the patient for therapy, and he's been complaining of side effects since he started the medicine. It makes sense to explore other medications. Anyway, Dr. Sutliff's return voice mail was totally demeaning. He questioned my credentials, said he could handle his own patients, and suggested I stick to psychoanalyzing my clients and leave the meds to him. He couldn't have been more pompous!"

"Sounds just like him," Annie said with a laugh. "He's the hospitalist at Gordon Memorial. He's the only doctor I won't let my new students interact with. I take their input and give it to him myself. I got tired of my students, even the guys, ending their first clinical week in tears."

"What a charmer. He obviously loves his daughter, but that's about all I can say on the plus side. She also told me that her daddy lives here, but her mommy is in Indy."

"Yeah, there have been rumors he's divorced," Annie noted.

"He's only been in Gordon for a few months. At first, all the females on staff were flirting like crazy with him. Then his personality reared its ugly head, and they've backed off. Given the lack of eligible men in Gordon, that says a lot."

Chapter Two

Mike was silent as he drove the Sutliff clan to his home. What was wrong with his parents? He'd told them repeatedly Sophie needed to be watched closely. Her impulsive behavior had worsened since the divorce, and she often went "exploring" in public places. His x-wife, Anita, had begun to hint that Sophie was becoming a source of conflict between her and Grant, her new husband. Mike dared to hope Anita would give him full custody of Sophie but doubted it would happen. Anita liked to win too much to give Sophie up. He also had to admit that Anita loved Sophie as much as he did.

Mike thought about the woman who had been walking Sophie back to the starting gate. Kristen was cute, kind of tall, with crazy, blondish hair. Who had hair that curly these days? It worked for her, though. She was wearing loose running shorts and a large, tie-dyed T-shirt. Her face glistened with sweat, despite being unable to finish the whole course.

She sounded like a psych text, Mike thought as he recalled Kristen's comments about Sophie. Memories of his last encounter with a mental health practitioner flooded back. He and Anita had failed marriage counseling. Miserably.

Remembering his retreat from Kristen, which was exactly what it was, Mike gave himself a mental scolding. His interactions with women continued to be at best ineffective, and at worst offensive. He'd have to work on that, once he figured out how to deal with his feeling of being in an alien universe. Nothing seemed right. None of the pieces of his life seemed to fit anymore.

Once home, his mother hurried to help Sophie clean up and change her dirty clothes. It was obvious Jane was also avoiding Mike. His father followed Mike to the kitchen, where they both began to prepare dinner.

"How are you doing, son?" Luke asked. "We sure didn't have the Independence Day we expected. But it all turned out fine."

"I don't know, Dad," Mike sighed. "No matter what I do, Sophie changes all my plans. I was convinced this weekend would be different, that she and I would be relaxed and have fun together. I know you and Mom did your best to watch her, but short of installing a GPS chip on her, I'm at a loss."

Luke laughed. "Well, you don't remember what a hyper kid you were at that age. Trust me, your mom and I were at our wits' end about half the time. But you grew out of it, and so will Sophie."

"I hope so," Mike replied. "Anita wants to have Sophie evaluated for meds. I don't see it. They have their place, but I believe her behavior is more related to the divorce than to a disorder."

"I absolutely agree!" Jane said as she rushed into the kitchen. "Sophie is doing everything her six-year-old brain can think of to try to make her world normal again. She can't yet trust that things will be okay eventually. Different, but okay. How can a little girl know such a thing? We've got to give her time, not medicine. She's sound asleep, by the way, so dinner can wait awhile."

Implicit in his mother's outburst was her opinion of Anita's focus on a med evaluation. Jane and Anita had never become friends, despite their mutual love of little Sophie. When Mike and Anita ended their marriage, Jane let go of all pretense that she liked Anita.

"Mom, Anita's doing what she thinks is best. Despite our differences, she was, and is, a good mother. She's adjusting to a new marriage. Sophie isn't making it easy."

"I would think it's *Anita's* job to deal with her new husband," Jane said, reflecting her opinion of Anita's spousal abilities. "Sophie has her own tasks, like being a first-grader and sharing her mother with a virtual stranger."

Mike grinned at his mother's transparent defense of anything Sophie did. He had to admit he also enjoyed Jane's painting of Anita as the total villain in the scenario of his broken marriage. But he was too honest to let it go.

"Mom, Grant isn't a stranger. And Anita isn't the only one who made mistakes. I worked nonstop, through med school, then residency, then fellowship. She was a single parent for most of those years. Maybe I'm getting a taste of what she went through. Heaven knows she tried to tell me, but I was too focused on my studies and work to listen. I'm more and more aware of the loneliness she must have felt."

"Maybe," Jane said. "One thing we all have to work on is improving Sophie's judgment. If she'd told us she wanted to see you at the finish line, we would have waited there. She's so independent, but then again your father's already reminded you of where she gets that trait." Jane smiled and returned to being her usual loving self. "So, what are you two gourmands making for our holiday meal?"

"I want a cheeseburger," Sophie said softly. "I woked up all by myself. I'm hungry. Where's Kristen?"

Mike lifted Sophie into his arms, kissing her cheek. "You're still half asleep, honey. You're at Daddy's house with Grandma and Grandpa. Kristen lives in her own house."

"Will she have cheeseburgers?"

"I'm not sure what she's having, Sophie. We're having grilled chicken, turkey burgers, sweet corn, and a big salad. Sound good?"

"Turkey burgers sound gross, Daddy. But Mommy makes me take one bite of everything, so I'll try one. What are we having for dessert?"

"Fresh mixed berries with whipped cream," Mike said.

"Shortcake, too?" Sophie asked. Her big blue eyes signaled hope for a more substantive dessert.

"No cake tonight," Mike said firmly. "It's important to fill our bodies with good things and not too many sweets."

Jane rolled her eyes as she assessed Sophie's tiny frame. Mike got her message. A little sugar wouldn't hurt Sophie. Maybe his mother had a point.

"If you eat some of the turkey burger, maybe we can have some cookies with the strawberries," he said. Sophie's eyes lit up, and he marveled at how much he loved his little girl. When she left on Sunday evening, he'd once again have to ignore the gaping hole in his heart.

After the drama of the day, dinner was remarkably pleasant. Sophie detailed her fear at being lost, Kristen's rescue, and her sadness at Mike's not "winning the race." Luke and Jane used Sophie's account to add some loving but heavy-handed counsel about never leaving their side in public places.

"I know all about bad people," Sophie said. "We talked about them in kindergarten. But I knew Kristen was going to help me. She said she wouldn't touch me and told me to yell loud if I felt afraid. She kept me away from the runners. They were going fast."

Sophie's earnest belief in Kristen both pleased and bothered Mike. Her instincts about Kristen were sound, but Kristen was a good person. Not everyone was.

"Honey, you were right about Kristen. But your teachers at school have probably said some bad people can act like they're good, like they're your friends. That's why you need to stay with Grandma and Grandpa all the time. Okay?"

"Okay, Daddy," Sophie replied. "I get it."

"Enough talk about this trying day," Luke said. "I heard a rumor there are fireworks at the college quad tonight. Should someone who's only six be allowed to stay up for the festivities?"

"Yes, yes, yes," Sophie said, jumping in her chair. "I'll hold someone's hand all night. I won't move an inch, I promise!"

Gordon Community College was comprised of five brick buildings bordering a large quadrangle. The quad served as the student recreation center during the warm months, with makeshift activities like kite-flying, sun tanning, and picnics occurring from

May through September. Tonight's fireworks drew several hundred people, but with viewing spaces throughout campus, no one felt crowded.

As Mike, Sophie, and his parents settled in on their blanket, he looked around. It felt unsettling not to know anyone in his old hometown. His patients came and went from his hospital service. He rarely had a chance to establish an ongoing relationship with them.

Mike gazed up when he heard familiar laughter. Kristen was with a group of friends, eating watermelon and setting her blanket on a flat patch of grass. Her hair was done in soft waves, in contrast to the tight curls from earlier today. She wore a sleeveless cotton sundress and carried a denim jacket. Mike couldn't help comparing her to Anita's usual look, which included designer dresses and accessories.

But I told her to buy them, he thought. *I was never home, and it was a way to ease my guilt.*

Sophie, who never missed a beat, also heard the familiar voice. "Daddy, it's Kristen!" she said. "I think we should say hi, you know, to be polite. But it's your decision, Daddy. I won't go *anywhere* without you."

Mike wasn't sure if he should reward such blatant manipulation, but he chuckled at Sophie's attempt. He decided it wouldn't hurt to thank Kristen again, so he and Sophie walked over to her group. Annie saw him first, and he noticed her nudge Kristen.

"Kristen, it's your friend Sophie," the little girl yelled. "I told my daddy I would hold his hand if I could come over to see you."

Alerted by Annie's poke, Kristen smiled at Sophie while glancing cautiously at her father. "Hi, honey. How was your afternoon? I'll bet you were tired after the race."

"I was, and then I ate a turkey burger," Sophie said proudly. "I like cheeseburgers better, but I put lots of ketchup on it. And we had cookies with our fruit!"

"Sounds lovely," Kristen said, grinning at the little girl.

Mike could tell Kristen wasn't that impressed. He wondered

what her idea of a healthy holiday meal included. Or was she irritated by something else?

"Tell Sophie about your ribs," Annie said with a smirk.

"My mom had me make different sauces for the ribs," Kristen explained. "Then she wouldn't eat any of them! She wanted a cheeseburger, too."

"Your mom sounds interesting," Mike said. "What kind of sauces did you make?"

"There were four. One was heavy on the garlic. Another had honey and molasses. The other two were varying proportions of mustard, vinegar, and tomato puree. If you have a need for barbecue sauce, give me a shout."

Mike laughed. "Based on Sophie's assessment of my turkey burgers, extra sauce might be a good thing. I'll ask Annie for your recipes the next time I see her."

Kristen smiled, but was clearly unwilling to make more small talk. Jane stepped in.

"Kristen, tell me more about yourself. You saved our precious Sophie, after all. What do you do?"

"I teach psychology at GCC," Kristen said. "I also have a small private practice a couple of evenings a week. Sometimes I consult with local doctors about patients. And I sell my crafts, too." Her words were pleasant, but Mike sensed he was getting the stink-eye from the pretty psychologist.

"Oh my," Jane said. "When do you have time to run? Or sleep?"

"There's plenty of time," Kristen said with a smile. "My dog, Bernie, helps with my fitness. Doodles need lots of exercise, and by extension I get my share."

"You have a dog?" Sophie said with a jump as she tugged at her father's hand. "I want a doggy, but everyone says I can't have one yet. Maybe I could visit you and Bernie. Please?"

Mike sighed. "Sophie, we don't invite ourselves to visit others. Kristen is very busy, as she just told us. A dog can wait, especially since you need to learn to listen better."

Kristen, Annie, Jane, and Luke stared at Mike. He realized that once again, he'd been autocratic in his efforts to temper Sophie's impulsive request.

"Honey, I'm sorry if I sounded tough on you," he said. "I just don't want Kristen to feel pushed to have company."

"It's fine, really," Kristen said. "Maybe some weekend Bernie and I could meet you here at the quad. While Sophie plays with Bernie, you and I could discuss your approach to mental health concerns."

Totally befuddled, Mike was about to ask Kristen what she meant when Annie jumped in to ease the tension. "Or maybe you could meet at the DogTrot next weekend. Sophie, there will be lots of dogs to see. Bernie usually comes. Were you going to enter him, Kristen?"

"Hadn't thought about it yet," Kristen said, with a subtle glare in Annie's direction. "I'll probably bring Bernie. He's got such a sweet nature, and he loves to socialize with all the other dogs."

"Wonderful!" Jane said. "Sophie is with us again next weekend, so we can bring her. Honey, do you promise you'll stay with me and Grandpa?"

"I promise, cross my heart and hope to die," Sophie said seriously, as she crossed her entire chest.

Mike knew a last chance when he saw one. It was time to change his approach to Sophie. And to Kristen, before she pegged him as just another arrogant doctor.

"I have an idea," he said. "Mom and Dad could use a free weekend, so Sophie and I will come. After the DogTrot, we could have a picnic here at the quad. I'll be glad to bring the food and drinks, if you'll bring your barbecue sauces. Annie, you're invited, too."

"Thanks, but I have plans to see my cousins in Indianapolis," Annie said. "We have a girls' weekend each summer, complete with spa treatments and more restaurant food than is good for us. Then we shop for end-of-summer bargains."

"You'll be missed, but it sounds like you'll be having your own fun," Mike said. "Kristen, are you on board? Mom, are you and Dad okay with some free time?"

Mike's father chimed in before Jane could respond. "You bet, son. Sounds good to me."

"Me, too," Kristen said. "I'm glad to bring more than just sauces. How about something chocolate for dessert?"

"Yummy," Sophie said. "Daddy's not big on chocolate. Only fruit counts as dessert."

Mike smiled in defeat. "Thank you, Kristen. We'll look forward to your chocolate creation."

Anita's phone call Monday evening capped what had been an already trying day. The hospital was full, and by the end of his twelve-hour shift, Mike was spent. However, he knew better than to let the call go to voice mail. Time to face the music with Anita.

"What's this about Sophie getting lost at the race, Mike?" Anita asked. Her voice didn't sound mad, which was a switch. "I wish you'd have told me when you dropped her off."

"You're right," Mike said. "I meant to tell you, but she'd fallen asleep on the drive to Indy, and we both know how tough it is to get her back to sleep if she's awakened. I was trying to help by carrying her in to her bed, and I forgot to tell you about the race."

"That's okay," Anita said. "Thank goodness this Kristen person helped her find you and your parents. Do you think this incident is another reason to have Sophie evaluated? I'm at a loss about what to do next. Grant says we should at least take her to our family practitioner to see what he thinks."

Mike gritted his teeth but resolved not to let the conversation turn into the usual tug of war. Sophie's well-being was too important to rehash Grant's lack of child-rearing expertise.

"I'm concerned too, Anita," he said calmly. "But I'd like to give Sophie a little more time to adjust to our divorce before we consider medication. My move to Gordon probably came too soon after we split. She's had to adjust to us not living together, then to us living in different cities. It's a lot for a kid to take in. And after the scare at the race, her behavior was much better. She was so frightened at being lost that the message to stay with an adult got through to her."

Mike inhaled, hoping Anita would accept his input.

"I'll tell Grant," Anita said. "I agree with you. Since she's been back, Sophie has been more compliant. I'd say obedient, but that would be pushing it. Grant loves her too, despite what you may think. He was very upset at the thought of her wandering around the race course by herself."

"Thanks, Anita," Mike said, relieved. "I guess Sophie's lucky to have three adults who care for her so much." His statement was a subtle nod to Grant. It killed him to make it.

"All righty then. You sound tired, Mike. Are things at your new job going well?"

"It's fine," he responded. "Long days, but after seven of them, I get seven off. My biggest concern is the lack of follow through with my patients. I see them in the hospital, but that's it. They go back to their primary physician, and I'll never know how they did. Unless I run into them at the grocery, which happens a fair amount of the time here in Gordon."

"Well, you always said Indianapolis was too big for your taste," Anita said. "Small towns have their downsides, too."

"True, I did say that. And I still believe it. I guess I'm a small-town guy at heart."

"I'll let you go," Anita said. "Just keep me posted on Sophie's weekends with you, okay?"

"Will do. Give Grant my best," Mike said. He was determined to be gracious. *Ugh.*

Luke and Jane had picked Sophie up while he ended an overnight shift. After exchanging updates on Sophie, Mike wished his parents a pleasant, child-free weekend. Luke gave Mike a wink as they left the house.

Sophie started in without taking a breath. "Daddy, do we get to dress up for the DogTrot?" she asked with hope in her high-pitched voice. "I have a pretty new dress from Grandma with doggies on it."

"How fancy is it?" Mike wondered, as he looked at his precious girl. "I think you'd be more comfortable in shorts and a top."

"I'm comfortable in my dress, Daddy," Sophie said, unwilling to give up her new outfit.

"Let's wear the dress another time, honey," Mike said firmly. Hearing no argument, he silently rejoiced at Sophie's lack of response. She was a stubborn little thing, but as his parents reminded him frequently, so was he.

Sophie changed and entered the room wearing orange shorts and a flowered shirt. She looked every inch a princess, despite her frown. "It's just not fancy enough, Daddy," she whined. "I should look pretty for all the dogs and puppies."

"You look wonderful," Mike said kissing Sophie's head. "How about if we fancy things up with a bow instead of a barrette?" He marveled at his new expertise in female headgear, expertly fastening the bow above Sophie's ear.

They bundled their supplies into the car, Sophie helping with the lighter snack bags of dried fruit and nuts. Mike handled the cooler, filled with containers of low-fat chicken salad, organic potato salad, and almond milk. He wondered if this was enough to fill Sophie up; his mother continued to comment on her thin frame. Maybe Kristen would bring food too. She had promised a chocolate dessert, hadn't she?

What was he thinking anyway? Kristen had been practically forced into accepting Sophie's request to picnic after the DogTrot. He'd teased her about bringing barbecue sauce after she'd talked about her mother's picky taste. He certainly didn't need her help to feed his daughter. But he wondered what she would eat at a picnic – given her devotion to running, she'd likely eat healthy like him. *Not that it mattered!*

After parking at the college lot, Mike and Sophie made their way to the starting line of the DogTrot. The course was the mile oval comprising the GCC track, with the center area reserved for those wanting to picnic during or after the trot. They deposited their sacks and coolers and spread out his mother's old quilt, establishing their space. As he made sure everything was in order, Sophie jumped and waved. Kristen had obviously arrived.

"Hi, Kristen," she said, with a joyful tone Mike hadn't heard from his daughter in a while. "Come and put your things with ours. Is that Bernie? Can I pet him?"

"Yes, this is the great Bernie," Kristen said with a laugh. "Of course you can pet him. If you don't, he'll mope for the rest of the afternoon. Hold your hand out, and he'll sit for you."

Bernie was on his best behavior. Soon he was on his back, tongue hanging to one side while Sophie rubbed his belly. Mike noticed Kristen's happy grin as she watched Bernie and Sophie get acquainted.

"He's a good dog, huh?" he asked Kristen.

"He's got a great personality," Kristen replied. "He's never met a stranger, always thinks today is the best day of his life, and he enjoys protecting me from whatever is behind the front door. My pizza delivery guy still won't come in, and I've lived at my place for a couple of years."

Pizza? Thought she was a healthy eater. Surely she respected her body enough that pizza was a rare treat. "Maybe he doesn't deliver too often," Mike said hopefully.

"No, nearly every Friday," Kristen said. "I enjoy kicking back when the week is over. No cooking on a Friday night, ever!"

"Speaking of food, you didn't have to bring anything," Mike said, looking at Kristen's large picnic basket. "We've got lunch covered."

"I didn't bring much. Surely you didn't think I'd just bring sauces from last week! I've got fried chicken legs, macaroni salad with bacon and cheese, and cherry brownie bars. What we don't eat, I'll bring for work lunches next week."

"That sounds very delicious," Sophie said, as her mouth watered.

"We just have some low-fat stuff, with nuts and wrinkly fruit for dessert."

"Rude, little one," Mike scolded. "Our food is tasty and good for you at the same time."

"I know, Daddy," Sophie said. "But I haven't had fried chicken since Easter at Grandma's."

"You'd think we didn't feed her," Mike said, as he wondered why he wanted to convince Kristen he was a good father. "She's thin like I was as a kid."

"No need to explain," Kristen said, as she smiled at Sophie. "Kids usually want what they don't have; maybe the same as adults! Anyway, everything in moderation, I always say."

"I think the latest guidelines are pretty clear about the value of low-fat, low-calorie living," Mike said. Instantly regretting his superior tone, he tried to backpedal. "You're right, though, about moderation. Look at the Mediterranean diet. Huge variety, plenty of olive oil, with wine to round it out."

Mike focused on Sophie and Bernie, who were practically lying in each other's arms. His daughter was certainly a dog lover. He'd have to play his cards carefully, or he'd be dealing with a puppy soon. But maybe that wasn't such a bad thought; Anita would have to let Sophie stay with him more often if there was a dog to play with. Wow, he was sure getting crafty in his old age, using a puppy to entice his daughter away from his ex and her husband.

"Looks like folks are lining up for the trot," he said. "Let's get over there so we can listen carefully to the instructions, Sophie."

Kristen lent her support. "Good idea, Mike. With all these dogs around, they'll probably stagger the start so the pooches aren't making friends instead of walking around the track."

"Making friends?" Sophie said with disgust. "Some of these doggies are smelling other dogs' butts. Double yuk."

"Dogs do a lot by smell, honey," Mike said. "One of my buddies from med school used to say when he let his dog out in the back yard each morning, the dog would sniff the entire yard, to see what and who had been around overnight. He said it was like us reading a newspaper, catching up on the latest events."

"You know that makes no sense," Sophie said with a haughty air. "Kristen, Bernie wouldn't smell a butt, would he?"

"Sorry, Sophie, but he sure would. It's gross, isn't it?" Kristen chuckled, and they made their way to the starting line.

The trot commenced, with Sophie, Mike, and Kristen ambling along as Bernie pranced with his tail high. At the half-mile mark, Sophie was obviously tired, and Mike suggested they cut through the grassy oval to have lunch.

"Perfect, Daddy," Sophie said. "I want to try Kristen's fried chicken and macaroni."

Kristen grinned sympathetically at Mike. "Why don't we all try some of everything," she said to Sophie. "That way we'll know more about what we like and don't like."

"I'm sure I don't like chicken salad, but I'll try some," Sophie countered.

Kristen praised the low-fat chicken and organic potato salad, while Sophie gobbled down two chicken legs. Mike looked at his daughter in wonder. Sophie had somehow gotten a grease stain on her bow, but she was certainly relishing her food. He'd thought she didn't have much of an appetite. Maybe he'd been wrong.

The cherry brownie bars were also a hit with his little girl. What was this about? Could Sophie be hungrier than she let on? Would she get fat on this sort of food if he let her eat what she wanted? Where was all his medical knowledge? He loved her so much; he wanted only the best for her. Maybe it was time to do more research on childhood nutrition.

"What a wonderful day for a dog walk and a picnic," Kristen said, as she sat back with Bernie laying a protective paw over her leg. "I haven't felt this relaxed in a while."

"Why can't you relax, Kristen?" Sophie asked, scrunching her face. "Do you worry a lot? My daddy says to trust in God, and things always work out."

"Your daddy's smart, isn't he?" Kristen replied. "I don't worry too much, though lately I've been thinking about my mom. My dad died in January, and my mom just moved to Arizona. I'm not sure if she should have, but we'll see. My sister lives near her, so that's a good thing."

Sophie patted Kristen's arm and snuck in a stroke to Bernie's back. "You and your mommy will be in my prayers, Kristen. It will be okay."

Mike noticed Kristen's teary gaze as she smiled at Sophie. Kristen had more going on in her carefree single life than he'd assumed. Her kindness to Sophie and devotion to her family were touching. He found himself wanting to know her better but doubted she'd be responsive to his interest. It was time to say something, but his usual clinical expertise had left the grounds.

"I'm sorry about your father, Kristen," he said. "That kind of grief is tough; maybe your mom thinks she can escape it with a change of scene."

"Exactly right, Mike," Kristen said, clearly in control of her emotions now. "I appreciate your sympathy. Every time I think I've got a handle on my sadness, a client or student will talk about their own losses, and I feel I haven't made any progress at all."

"Time is the best tincture, as the old docs used to say," he replied. "Sounds trite, but there's truth there. Six months is no time when you're dealing with the loss of someone dear to you."

Kristen smiled gratefully, arching her brow. "You're very psychologically minded, Dr. Sutliff," she said. "Your patients probably benefit from your combination of empathy and kindness. This is in direct opposition to what I previously thought of your clinical skills."

Mike laughed. "Don't go getting all mushy on me, Kristen. My reputation, as Annie has probably told you, is one of grizzly bear toughness, not touchy-feely sweetness."

"No, you've given yourself away. You may be tough on students, but my sense is you're very empathetic with your patients."

"Hold on," Mike countered. "What did you think was wrong with my clinical skills? Where did that come from?"

"I should confess. I'm the Dr. Anderson who left you a message about the antidepressant switch for one of your patients. You gave me quite a scolding in your return message."

Mike wondered how to communicate with this intriguing woman. He was careful with his response. "I do remember your call now. I was at the end of a twelve-hour stint, and I'd just seen the patient in question. He'd already told me about his side effects and your concerns. Mentally, I was done. Sorry if I was overbearing."

"Oh, you were definitely overbearing. There are many other words I'd use to describe your manner, but we're in the presence of a tender six-year-old."

"What-EVER," Sophie said. "This is so boring. Can I throw the ball to Bernie while you guys talk? I'll stay right by the tree with red buds, so you can see me. And I'll yell loud if anyone bugs me."

"Fine," Mike said. "But watch your attitude, young lady. It's rude to announce that you're bored."

Sophie smiled and kissed her father's cheek as she and Bernie headed to the tree. "As you can see, I've got an iron discipline thing going on with her," Mike said with a sheepish half-smile.

Kristen laughed, shaking her head. "You and Sophie clearly adore each other," she said. "She's lucky to have you as a dad. I hear lots of parenting horror stories. You two are wonderful together."

"Thanks," Mike said as he gathered trash from their picnic. "I've made my share of mistakes, though. My parents have such a happy marriage, and I was sure mine would be the same. Too bad I didn't factor in the crazy demands of med school and beyond. Anita just got tired of being alone, especially after Sophie was born. I couldn't understand why she'd quit on us, especially when I was so close to the prize. But the toll of ten years of medical training was too much. I often wonder what I'd do differently – maybe giving couples counseling more time would have helped."

"I sense you're not convinced it would have mattered," Kristen said. "I'm sorry it didn't work for you and Anita. I truly believe in the power of counseling, but there are no guarantees. Too many variables. And obviously, both partners have to be willing to do the hard work of therapy." She took a breath and continued. "Did Sophie say Anita had remarried? That adds to the mix, huh?"

"You think?" Mike snorted. "Sorry, that was rude, and I just chided Sophie for the same behavior. Grant is an okay guy, but it galls me to see Sophie spend so much time with him and Anita. And since I moved back to Gordon, our weekend visits are decreased by the drive time to and from Indy."

"To be honest," he continued, "Grant is more than an okay guy. He's a good person, spent many years as a single, and he's thrilled to have Anita and Sophie in his life. But he's had this bug in his ear lately to have her evaluated for ADHD, which I'm not sure about. Sophie can be a handful, but I think she's still normal in terms of her behavior."

"I've only met Sophie a few times," Kristen said. "Based on what I've seen, I think I'd attribute her impulsivity to adjustment issues for now. You can always consider the eval later if you need to."

Mike was surprised at the wave of gratitude flooding through him. More than gratitude, actually. He felt appreciation and attraction. Kristen looked earnest, caring, and quite pretty as she discussed Sophie. He noticed her scent as well – something sweet and floral, but not cloying. Just like her. She was direct with her assessment of his treatment of depressed patients, and she may have implied he'd taken the easy way out of marriage counseling. Good grief. Was he becoming interested in this opinionated teacher/psychologist/crafter?

Chapter Three

Kristen peered at the contents of her craft closet and tried to decide which project she would work on today. After this morning's DogTrot, complete with Sophie's endearing comments of faith and Mike's revelations about his marriage, she felt the need for a mindless task. She needed to process all she'd heard, along with the unsettling feelings she had experienced. Mike Sutliff had affected her strongly. No one since Rob had caused her to ruminate about a man this much. Maybe it was Sophie, though. She was a real cutie.

Should she work on grapevine wreaths for the holiday season? No, she didn't want to risk burning herself with hot glue. That happened often enough, even when she wasn't preoccupied. Sew linens to coordinate with the hodge-podge tea sets she'd compiled from the most recent garage sales? Maybe. Sewing appealed to her right now. Then she saw it – the old pastel quilt she'd scored for only three dollars because it had a big rip in the center. It would make several adorable teddy bears. Kristen had made so many in the past, she could almost put them together blindfolded.

She had the bear cut out in barely fifteen minutes. Sewing the pieces together took about the same amount of time. Kristen grabbed the bag of stuffing (bought on sale with double coupons during the Fourth of July weekend) and filled the legs, arms, and head. Those appendages were attached to the body, which was then stuffed to rounded perfection. Hand sewing finished off the bear's back seam. The final product looked darling, she had to admit. Now the fun part – how to decorate Mr. or Ms. Bear. Her craft closet yielded remnants of lace and ribbon, just the right sizes for a collar and bow.

Looking closely, Kristen decided that this bear needed nothing else. The quilt pattern had fallen perfectly to give the illusion of eyes and a pert mouth, making it an ideal gift for a new baby. There were no buttons to cause choking, allowing her to price the bear even more competitively.

As she worked, Kristen wondered about Mike's account of his marriage and divorce. She felt sad, and somewhat doubtful, about his description of Anita's unhappiness. Hadn't they both known what they were getting into when Mike entered med school? Were they both so naïve they assumed the stressors wouldn't impact them? Couldn't they have found their way around their isolation and anger, so Sophie could grow up with both parents?

But based on his condescending message after her request for a medication consult, she could understand how his marriage went south. Mike was the kind of man who was two-hundred percent sure of himself, no matter what the circumstances. His poor x-wife must have had quite a time dealing with an absent husband and raising little Sophie on her own.

Chiding herself, she realized how judgmental she was. She and Rob should have been able to work through their differences, but they hadn't. Sometimes things just didn't work out. Mike spoke of Anita with affection, which was a good sign based on Kristen's work with divorced couples. And Sophie was a child brimming with faith, surprising Kristen with her trust in God and promise to pray for Kristen and her mommy.

That faith thing was another concern for Kristen. When she'd worked at the mental health center with Lauren, her friend's faith had grounded her during many a tough time. But Kristen couldn't quite get it. She believed in some sort of higher being, she supposed, but praying was beyond her. Her father had been a regular at Sunday services, and look what had happened to him. The doctors had said he was cured, then another ailment killed him. Kristen knew she was being childish; bad things happened to everyone. But reconciling all that with faith was too much for her.

Mike's affection for his x-wife was also bothersome. Maybe he wasn't truly over her. Lots of divorced couples reunited after marrying another partner. She sure didn't want to get in the middle of that scenario. Not that there was anything to be in the middle of!

Startled by the ring of her phone, Kristen hurried to the living room to answer. It was Katie, her sister in Arizona. Hopefully this was a social call, not one related to their mother.

"Hey, Katerpie, what's up?" Kristen teased, fingers crossed. "How are you doing with that hundred-degree dry heat?"

"It beats Indiana snow any day," Katie shot back. "How are you doing? Anything new in Gordon? How many jobs do you have? Seriously, I worry about you with all your different irons in the fire."

"Funny, Sis. I still have my teaching, private practice, and crafting. You interrupted the last of the three. What's new at your end?" Kristen could tell Katie wasn't calling to chat. Despite her banter, her sister's tone was tense.

"Nothing to worry about, I hope. I talked to Mom today, and she said a few things I need to run by the family psych expert. Like, she's been buying lots of things on the television shopping channels. Stuff she doesn't need. Jewelry, new sheets, pots and pans. And according to the activities director at her apartment, she's not been coming to bingo or any of the community outings. Mom's not one to isolate herself, so I'm running it by you."

"I'm glad you told me, Katie," Kristen said. "My initial instinct is that Mom's grief is finally hitting her hard now that the initial rush of moving to Arizona is past. Have you asked her about any of this?"

"Not yet. I was hoping you would call her and feel her out. I'm an insurance adjustor, not a shrink."

"No, you're a chicken," Kristen chided. "I'll call her tomorrow. We usually connect on Sundays anyway, so it won't look contrived. I'll get back to you after we talk."

"Thanks, Kristen," Katie said with a sigh. "You're a great big sister. By the way, how are you really doing? I didn't mean to be nasty about all your jobs. Are you making ends meet?"

"Things are okay for now," Kristen answered. "GCC has forecasted increased enrollments for the fall, so I've got another year of good salary and benefits. And Annie introduced me, sort of, to the new doctor in town. He's got all the girls alternately excited and running for cover."

Kristen spent the next several minutes filling Katie in on Mike, Sophie, and the details of their recent contacts. "Sis, you'd better watch yourself," Katie said. "You've always had a soft spot for a lonely kid with a hunky dad. But then, who doesn't?"

"This dad *is* hunky, but he's got so many personality quirks it could take decades to smooth them out. I'm pretty sure I don't need that kind of grief."

After the sisters ended the call Kristen found herself feeling lonely. Her pride in the completed teddy bear was gone, replaced by the familiar ache of anxiety about the future. What was going on with her mother? She'd always been a little flighty, but never a spendthrift. Kristen mentally crossed her fingers that grief was the primary culprit, but she had to admit the possibility of early dementia had entered her thoughts.

Nothing could be done right now. Kristen realized she was hungry. It was past seven and she hadn't eaten since she'd forced herself to rave over Mike's low-fat chicken salad at the DogTrot. She wondered how people could think fake mayo tasted anywhere as good as the real deal, complete with egg yolk, drizzled oil, and the perfect seasoning blend. Oh well.

A quick search of her pantry and refrigerator yielded little of substance – eggs, past-date milk, wrinkled carrots, and some cheese. Her freezer was full, but she was too tired to defrost burger and cook. Time for the grocery store.

Later, on her way to check out, she surveyed her finds. The basics were there: milk, gourmet cheese, and fresh vegetables. She'd also added some "fun food," favorites from her childhood. French onion dip, barbecue potato chips, cheese doodles, and the assortment of cookies from the bakery almost caused her to drool. Who said good nutrition had to be boring? Even Mike said balance was the key. Her cart was definitely balanced. Maybe. Perhaps the scale was tilted a little heavy toward fat and sugar.

And speaking of Mr. Balance, suddenly there he was smiling at her, but sneakily surveying her cart. “Interesting selection, Kristen. I see you’re a more complex woman than I’d thought. Which of these will you be feasting on tonight; the items that need to be washed and peeled, or the ones with all the additives?”

“Funny, Dr. Sutliff,” Kristen said, resolving to stay cool. “Where’s your better half, that is, Sophie?”

“She’s with my parents, talking endlessly about Bernie, the world’s most perfect dog,” Mike replied, still grinning. “I thought I’d do a quick grocery run without her input.”

“Okay, I’ll play,” Kristen said. “Judging by the food in *your* cart, I’d say you’re good for twelve, maybe twenty-four hours at best. All this stuff will rot soon.” She was exaggerating, but not by much. The produce items were fresh, ripe or past, and required extensive preparation before they could be consumed. No wonder Sophie was so thin!

Mike looked pained and was forced to agree. “You make a point, Kristen. I’m worried about Sophie’s health, and she sure loved your picnic offerings. What foods would you add to my cart to appeal to her? Bear in mind I’m a curmudgeon, and not easily convinced of the error of my ways.”

Kristen laughed loudly, startling the other shoppers. “Well spoken, Mike. Here’s what I’d do. Don’t inundate Sophie with junk food, but don’t restrict it so severely either. You don’t want her trading her ‘healthy’ lunches for some other kid’s convenience foods. I’d start with some organic macaroni and cheese, and maybe one package of cookies with minimal additives. I’ll bet she’ll develop food preferences, as we all do, and will gravitate to a wide variety of foods. I guess I’m saying you don’t want her to think there are ‘good’ or ‘bad’ foods – just foods that will both feed our bodies while still giving us pleasure.”

As Mike stared at her, Kristen wondered what he thought of her lengthy speech. Whatever. She'd been honest, and he had asked for feedback on his selections.

"You're right, much as I hate to admit it," he said. "Since med school, I've been all about caring for our bodies as the temples God made them to be. But my mother recently reminded me I survived during my grade school years on a diet of tacos and cheese pizza. For breakfast I would eat only one brand of sugared corn flakes. She thought I was going to develop every vitamin deficiency known to man."

"You're fine, and Sophie will be, too," Kristen said. Taking a breath, and a risk, she continued. "I have a proposition, Dr. S. Why don't you come for dinner sometime, and I'll cook what I think are both nutritious and fun foods? You can judge for yourself."

"Sophie will be at her mother's for the next ten days, while I work my seven-on rotation. If the invitation is open to just me, I'd be glad to come. If you wanted Sophie, we'll have to postpone." Mike looked closely at Kristen. She couldn't tell if he wanted her to withdraw the invite or include him alone.

"You're welcome to come solo," she said, wondering at her sanity. "Sophie has already given my food her stamp of approval. How about next Saturday evening at eight? Will you be too tired?"

"That's perfect," Mike said with a huge smile. "By the end of the week I'm tired, but mostly tired of cooking for one. It will give me something to look forward to. Can I bring anything?"

At that offer, both of them hooted. "No, the idea is that I cook and you pass judgment, remember? That's a strength of yours, as I recall," Kristen said. "I'll handle everything."

Sunday dawned and after walking Bernie, working in her tiny vegetable garden, and catching up on laundry, Kristen was ready to tackle the weekly phone call to her mother. Despite repeated efforts and several voice mails, her mom wasn't answering her phone. Kristen placed a casual but concerned call to the apartment manager and was told in an automated message that she was on vacation for the next two weeks. By the time she reached the administrator on call, she felt she'd overreacted to her mother's silence.

"I saw Mrs. Anderson just yesterday at lunch," Gayle, the administrator, said. "She ate well and told me to compliment the chef. I remember because so many times I'm told by residents to tell the chef that things weren't right – the food was cold, too spicy, and so on. And she pulled her awake switch this morning, so she's up for the day."

"Well, thanks," Kristen said. "Maybe Mom just forgot to charge her phone. It's an older model, so perhaps the battery is done for. My sister and I are grateful for all the good care Mom receives at your facility, Gayle. Have a good day."

Kristen enjoyed her Monday, despite the usual grumblings about how she'd graded the last exam's essay questions. Summer courses were compressed, and students either thrived with the intense schedule or gave up early on. One of Kristen's success stories this summer was Max, a classic underachiever, who had taken Kristen's dare when he asked her to sign his drop form. In return for his regular visits to the campus Writing Center, she had agreed to allow him to rewrite his first term paper. One-on-one tutoring at the WC yielded a fine essay on parent-child bonding in addition to another referral for dyslexia testing; both she and Max were proud of the result. He'd even told her how glad he was he hadn't dropped the course – for the usually shy student, Max's admission was a *big deal.*

She enjoyed her Monday until office hours. As Kristen sorted through the latest batch of emails, Heather, a senior student with a perfect GPA, appeared at the door.

"Dr. Anderson, can I have a minute?" she asked, not waiting for an answer as she sat in the chair by Kristen's desk. "We need to discuss your evaluation of my exam response to the prompt about Freud's theory of psycho-sexual development."

"We do?" Kristen asked, arching her brow and eyeing Heather's arm on her desk. "*I'm* not in need of a discussion at this point."

"Okay, I came on a little strong," Heather countered, putting her hand in her lap. "But your comment that my discussion was 'barely scratching the surface' of Freud's thinking was pretty harsh."

"Heather, read your essay aloud and pretend it was a response from a Psych 101 student."

After reading her essay as instructed, Heather said, "It's very good, don't you think? I covered all the primary points of the theory and summarized them well."

"That you did," Kristen said. "But you did it as a student would in an intro course, not in senior level *Theories of Psychotherapy*, which happens to be the course in which you're enrolled. If you reread the prompt, it said to describe the theory and then apply it to a clinical case."

Kristen hated the haughty tone she was using, but Heather seemed to bring that out in her. "Heather, it's a good response to the first part of the prompt, but you ignored half the task. And I know you well enough to be sure you've got more insight than this answer shows. What's going on with you?"

Despite her aversion to Heather's grade grubbing, Kristen liked the young woman and respected her intellectual abilities. Heather looked tired, was wearing the same wrinkled top as yesterday, and seemed a touch thinner than when the summer course began two weeks ago. Kristen's clinical radar was pinging.

"Nothing's going on!" Heather cried as she stood up. "You graded my test unfairly, and Max told me about your special treatment for him. You're not offering me the same chance to redo my essay. Your sense of fairness seems to be pretty variable – and it's weighted heavily in favor of male students. I'll be taking this issue to the department chair, since you obviously don't want to hear my side of things."

Heather stomped out of Kristen's office, leaving her in teacher shock. What had just happened? In the past she and Heather had gotten along well. Kristen seemed to strike the right balance between pushing Heather to do her best versus being a sounding board for her numerous complaints about her family. Radar still pinging loudly, Kristen thought about her next step.

She decided to connect with her department chair, Dr. Debra Stevens, who was seasoned in the ways of senior psych majors competing for the best graduate school offers. As they talked in Kristen's office, Debra also wondered about Heather's outburst. "I've noticed similar things, Kristen. One of the advantages of being on the faculty of a small community college is that we get to know our students well. Heather's been inattentive in my senior seminar, and as you said she's been wearing the same clothes repeatedly. What's your plan to get her to the Counseling Center?"

"No plan in place yet," Kristen said. "I'm glad, or not really glad but you know what I mean, that you've seen similar changes in Heather. Her behavior seems to be more than typical grad school anxiety, though. Maybe she'll open up more next week when midterms come out."

"We'll see," Debra said. "Heather's parents used to call me regularly. They were the prototypical 'helicopter parents,' but they've been silent for a while. I thought that was a good sign, but maybe not."

"Heather was also upset by her perception that I'd given Max special treatment. I couldn't tell her I'd referred him to the Writing Center as a way to eventually get him evaluated for learning disabilities. I knew Max had excellent verbal comprehension of the material when we discussed topics in class, but his written work was a disaster." Kristen looked away, worried about Debra's reaction.

"I can understand how Heather felt you were playing favorites," Debra said, tapping her pen on her forehead. "Of course, you weren't, and due to confidentiality rules, you couldn't reveal the full story. I'll back you up when she brings her complaint to me, but I think she'll go on to the dean if she has to."

"The dean hasn't been too friendly the few times we've met,"

Kristen said. "What's your take on how he handles student complaints?"

"He's been very student-centered in my experience. But as I said, I'll back you up, and I'll explain your work with Max. Still, try to approach Heather in the meantime. Maybe she'll let you know what's changed in her life."

Kristen's anxiety ticked up. "By student-centered, do you mean the dean's unfair to faculty?"

"Not exactly." Debra paused, then continued in a quiet voice after checking to be sure the door was shut. "I think he's just trapped by the usual dean responsibilities. Enrollments are tricky, parents are vocal, and he's in the middle when things get hot."

"I thought fall enrollments were projected to be good," Kristen said. "Isn't that true?"

"We'll see in August," Debra hedged. "I've heard nothing official, but my best source from administration says it could be a lean academic year."

As Kristen left for the day, she stewed about the conflict between being a mental health practitioner and a teacher. If Heather were a psychotherapy client, Kristen would have forged a bond early on, learning about Heather's background and history. That fund of knowledge would have allowed her to use some gentle confrontation now. But she was Heather's professor, not her counselor. Unless Heather was suicidal or homicidal, Kristen couldn't breach those boundaries without using extreme care. Heather didn't seem to be a danger to anyone, but she was very angry about something. Given her unkempt appearance, which was a marked change from her usual meticulous grooming, Heather was in trouble of some sort.

Carrying in the mail as she greeted Bernie, her "handsome boy," Kristen's phone rang. The ID said it was her mother. *Time for a showdown, as if I haven't had my share already today.*

"Mom, where have you been?" Kristen asked, knowing she was putting her mother on the defensive. "I've been really worried."

"Yes, I know," Kaye Anderson said, the chill traveling through space to frost Kristen's ear. "Checking up on me as if I were a child. I was mortified when the weekend administrator left a message with the director about your calls. Do you want me to get kicked out of here?"

Knowing her mother's skill at diversion, Kristen wasn't sidetracked. "No one gets kicked out for missed phone calls, Mom. Was your phone dead? Did you forget to charge it? I do that often, as do many people. As I said, it's not a serious offense."

Kristen's attempt to lighten the mood went nowhere. Her mother ranted on. "I have a life, you know. As it happens, I had a guest and thought it best to return my calls later. There's really no issue to discuss."

"A guest? I'm glad to hear you're making new friends, Mom. What's her name?"

"His name is Nolan, dear," her mother said. "And before you get overly protective, he's a wonderful man. We have so much in common – we like the same music, television shows, and he even likes to play miniature golf here on the grounds. Your dad's been gone several months, Kristen. I hope you're able to understand."

There it is, Kristen thought. *Never would I ever have seen this coming. So much for my clinical radar. And I need to watch my ageism, too. Mom is bound to have romantic interests. She's still a relatively young woman.*

"Well, that's great, Mom," Kristen said, almost slurring her words. "You deserve a wonderful man in your life, just like Dad was. Maybe you could introduce him to Katie the next time she picks you up for a shopping trip."

"Your sister wouldn't give Nolan a fair shake," Kaye countered. "You know what a daddy's girl she was. She wants me to be alone for the rest of my life."

Suddenly Kaye's tone changed. "I know you're worried I'll do something silly, honey. It's not like that. I just feel so alone, and it's nice to talk to someone my own age for once. Someone who isn't bragging about her newest purse or their daughter's latest romance."

As was usually the case, Kristen felt poked by her mother, just as she had thought the conversation was going to be more substantial, more heartfelt. Since she didn't have a new romance to discuss, she let it go. "Mom, I guess I haven't been able to see things from your perspective. If Nolan's a good guy, that's what Katie and I want for you. If not, I'll come to Arizona and use my karate skills to make him sorry."

"No need, honey," Kaye said, obviously relieved at Kristen's lighthearted tone. "I can take care of myself. Or maybe I should say I'm learning to do that. I've realized how great your dad was, and how much I took him for granted. I miss him so."

Kristen let the conversation veer to small talk after that. Her mother seemed to be thinking rationally. What had she and Katie expected – that their mother would live alone for the rest of her life? But not answering calls was a different matter, one Kristen would bring up during her next conversation with her mother.

After a light dinner of grilled chicken and salad, Kristen decided she'd had enough of scholarly activities for the day. Grading papers could wait, as could her email messages. And she sure wouldn't be solving much in terms of her mother's grief for now.

Her own grief struck her as she looked out at the maple tree in her yard, the tree her father had helped her plant when she bought her home. Tears welled up, streaming down her cheeks. She fought memories of her dad's teasing humor, his encouragement when she decided to pursue her Ph.D., and his love for her mother. Somehow thinking about his kind nature made her even sadder. Was there any hope she would find a man like her dad? Then she choked back a combination laugh and sob; was all the talk about Freud's theory coloring how she grieved? Did she have a "daddy complex" a la Freud?

There was only one thing to do when she was this morose. It was time for crafting, and based on Debra's assessment of fall enrollment, Kristen might need to sell more teddy bears than she'd planned.

Yesterday's bear seemed to look at her with a sly wink, despite having no eyes. Switching gears, she decided to work on a wreath. The sting of hot glue might bring her back into focus.

A twelve-inch wreath from last month's church tag sale was quickly denuded of its faded brown polyester flowers. Thinking about upcoming Christmas hobby shows, Kristen plunged into her craft closet for red, green, and white flowers and other baubles. Her stock was low, so she planned to make an off-center floral arrangement, accented with a plump gold bow. Faux holly berries would circle the rest of the wreath resulting in a simple, elegant creation.

Glue gun in hand, Kristen began attaching the berry sprigs. She made fast work of them, and then she carefully planned how she wanted to place the flowers for the fullest impression.

It's tough making it look full with so few stems, she thought. *I've got to replenish my stock or there won't be any income at all from the craft shows.*

When she'd done all she could with the wreath, and with only three glue burns, she decided to put her crafts aside. She needed to talk to someone, and Annie was always a good listener. Annie picked up on the first ring.

"What's up, friend?" Annie asked, with her usual good cheer. "We don't usually gab until our Friday night pizza date. Something wrong?"

"Nothing big, just lots of little life problems," Kristen said. She updated Annie on her disgruntled student, the shaky fall enrollments predicted for the psychology department, and her mother's new friend. "My counseling skills have left me, and I'm feeling out of sorts."

"You're in pain because you miss your father," Annie said. "If he were here, he'd remind you that things usually work out, though in ways we can't always predict. He'd lecture you with love, of course, and coach you to have more faith. Your mom will be fine; she's always been a survivor. But I know she's in real agony, too."

"Grief aside, what will I do if I get downsized to adjunct status?" Kristen asked. "When Lauren was worried about starting her private practice, she said she'd eat beans if she had to. I'm not sure that I'll even be able to afford beans!"

"Boy, are you in drama mode," Annie scolded. "As I just said, things will work out in ways you can't foresee. You can always see more clients and do more crafting. Sounds idyllic to me."

Kristen paused, then opened up with her latest concern. "Yes, I used to agree that things worked out, eventually. But isn't that an adolescent, lazy way of viewing the world? There's lots going on that won't ever work out – poverty, prejudice, cruelty. Annie, I'm not sure I can buy in to that blind faith in the world's goodness."

"Let's change the subject.," Annie said. "You make a point, but I'm too tired to debate faith or philosophy. Anything new with Dr. Mike?"

"As it happens, we ran into each other at the grocery. I invited him for dinner after he made fun of my food choices. He's still a bit of a peacock, but I can tell he loves Sophie. He's worried about her being too thin."

"He should be," Annie said. "I'd give that kid whatever she wanted to eat, even if she demanded pizza and gelato for breakfast. Of course, my Italian genes may be speaking for me. Skinny kids need my help."

Annie paused for a second. "But, what did you just say? You're having Dr. S for dinner? He teased you about your market items? This is very intriguing, Kristen. No wonder you're pondering the state of the world. You've been holding out on me. What are you going to make him for dinner?"

"Haven't a clue. You have given me a good idea about Italian food, though. I could go all Mediterranean diet on him. Didn't he mention it once?" Kristen tried to remember when Mike had talked about healthy living, though it was hard to pin down since that was a pretty consistent theme with him.

"He didn't mention it to me, girlie. I think you're stressing about more than just work and your mom. I haven't seen you this off-center in quite a while. And after Rob's stupidity, it's about time you got back in the game." Annie was never one to mince words, but Kristen appreciated her honesty.

"I think Mike Sutliff is the least of my worries, Annie. The last thing I need is a doctor who thinks he knows everything, even down to my nutritional status. Although if I lose my job and end up eating beans, he'll admire my healthy choices!"

Chapter Four

As he dressed, Mike wondered what he was about to experience. Dinner at the junk food queen's house? She was a runner, which he had to credit her for, but her grocery cart had been very telling. How on earth did she maintain her healthy weight?

Could I be more judgmental? he asked himself. After all, he couldn't get his six-year-old daughter to eat. His parents had better luck with her, though he knew they were giving Sophie foods he wouldn't approve of. What had Kristen said? Something about offering Sophie a few organic treats and letting her develop her own taste in food? It just seemed risky to him. Sophie's health was too important.

He hoped his choice of cargo shorts and a polo top was fancy enough for this dinner. He didn't know Kristen well, but he guessed she'd be an informal hostess. Since she was in charge of the food, he skipped his usual date offering of fresh fruit for dessert and took a bouquet of summer flowers out of the refrigerator. Surely she wasn't allergic to fresh flowers.

As he pulled up to Kristen's home, his clinical mindset assessed it carefully. Small, built in the fifties probably, in the usual mid-century modern style. It looked cozy though, with the potted plant on the miniscule porch. Her door was painted a bright blue, contrasting well with the beige brick and sandstone frontage. *Her house looks like her*, he realized. *Attractive, unpretentious, and welcoming.*

"Hi there," Kristen said, startling him as she opened the door. "I've got Bernie on a short leash, literally, so come in and prepare to be loved to death. I'll take the beautiful flowers before he ruins them."

Several doggie kisses later, and after Bernie had made several laps around the entire house, Mike caught his breath. He had been right about his clothing. Kristen was dressed in a casual sundress with a bright sweater. She was wearing those funky sandals that were cute enough but were supposedly good for your feet, her toes polished with a summery pink shade. All in all, she looked great, especially with her hair partially pulled back. And that floral scent hit him again. Very nice.

"Your home is great, Kristen," he said. "I was admiring the exterior when you came to the door. And your furniture reminds me of my parents' selections."

"Thanks, I think," Kristen said. "And thanks for the lovely flowers. My décor, as you noticed, is made up primarily of my mother's things after she downsized. My father's death rattled her, and she made some hasty decisions about disposing of her treasures, moving away, and so on. But I benefitted, as you can tell. I've refinished some of the pieces, but most are as they were during my childhood."

"I'm sorry about your dad," Mike said, remembering she'd mentioned it before. "How are you doing? Grief is a slow process."

"Very true, unfortunately. I'm okay. Some days are better than others. And life has a way of keeping me occupied so I don't dwell on missing my father."

"I'm blessed to have two living parents," Mike said. "I don't know what I'd have done without them when my marriage ended. They're crazy about Sophie. They help me more than I can say."

"Well, Sophie's a precious girl," Kristen said. "I'm sure they dote on her with no complaints. Anyway, are you ready for a delicious meal, made with ingredients that may cause you to do an herbal cleanse tomorrow?" She smiled, arching her brows.

Mike knew she was teasing and liked her for it. "I'm ready and willing. I predicted the menu on my drive over. I'm thinking some type of boxed helper made with high-fat ground beef, instant mashed potatoes, and frosted cake from a mix for dessert."

"That does sound delightful," Kristen said, not kidding, but smiling again. "It's one of my favorite go-to menus, especially after a tough day. Nothing says comfort more than noodles, potatoes, and sweets for dessert. But you're out of luck tonight, Mike. We're having Italian."

Trying unsuccessfully to hide his wince at the description of Kristen's favorite menu, Mike said, "Italian sounds good." He envisioned red sauce from a jar on top of bleached-flour pasta.

Kristen had the food set out buffet-style in her kitchen, and they carried their plates to her dining nook. Mike was surprised at the lightly breaded chicken cutlets, multi-colored pasta with a homemade wine sauce, and vegetable blend seasoned lightly with garlic and oil. Crusty bread completed the feast.

"This looks great, Kristen," he admitted. "And it tastes even better than it looks."

"Thank you," she replied. "You'll be glad to hear the chicken was cooked in extra virgin olive oil, and that the bread has very little butter. But wait for dessert – it's truly decadent."

"Somehow I knew that would be the case," he said. "Chocolate, I'm guessing?"

"No, not today. My culinary repertoire goes far beyond chocolate, though I'm not sure why anyone would want to venture away from it. Dessert is apple crisp topped with vanilla bean frozen yogurt."

"I haven't had apple crisp since I was little," Mike said. "It's kind of gone out of style."

"It was the first thing I learned to cook in 4-H. They hooked us on cooking by teaching us an easy, tasty dessert. Some of the new restaurants in Indianapolis are featuring fruit crisps, but they're still rare menu items."

As she cleared the dinner plates, Bernie made his usual opportunistic survey of the table and floor. "I call him my living vacuum," Kristen said. "I have to be careful what I leave on the stove top and in the sink. He'll eat anything, even soapy water!"

Mike watched Kristen's easy, graceful movements as she made her way around Bernie and the dinette set. He had to admit dinner had been wonderful. He felt pleasantly full, but ready for dessert. It occurred to him that after his usual meal of vegetables and bread, he was rarely full. Or at least not for long.

Kristen's approach to eating was foreign to him, but he was willing to give it a try. He realized he was not just attracted to Kristen's food, but to her approach to life. He sensed she'd had enough sadness for several people lately, but she soldiered on. He contrasted her response to his own after Anita left. He'd been angry, and still was, shutting others out and being suspicious of any female who was friendly. *Time to get over yourself, buddy*, he thought.

"Voila!" Kristen said as she put the dessert plates at their places. "Enjoy this fine dessert, which includes fruit, oats, butter, and dairy. Isn't it cool that almost all the food groups are represented?" Kristen waggled her brows, clearly mocking his near obsession with nutrition.

"Okay, I give," Mike said. "It's all been delicious. I'll grant you that excellent cuisine can coexist with good nutrition."

"Thanks for that, Mike. This is the sort of food I was talking about introducing Sophie to. It's good for her growing body, and she could have seconds if she wanted without you worrying she was being totally unhealthy. And maybe she wouldn't like it at all – that would be okay as long as she tried each item."

"Well, at least I've done that right," he said. "She's learned to try at least a bite of everything on her plate. After that, though, I'm not sure what to do. I don't want her going to bed hungry, so I usually let her have a bowl of cereal."

"She's definitely your daughter!" Kristen said with a laugh. "Didn't you tell me you'd only eat one type of cereal growing up? Do you let Sophie have the sugared flakes?"

"Touché," Mike said as he eased back in his chair. "What's your pleasure now? I have to be at the hospital tomorrow at seven, but I've got time for an after-dinner stroll. Would you and Bernie want to take a walk?"

"Great idea. Let's drive to the GCC quad. My neighborhood has a few unleashed dogs, and Bernie's had some bad experiences." Kristen had Bernie's walking lead on in no time, and he bounded into Mike's car as if he owned the vehicle.

"Hope you're not too picky about dog slobber and paw prints," Kristen joked. "I've got covers on my back seat, but they don't help all that much."

"Not a problem. I'm enjoying Bernie's company. Yours as well," Mike said, glancing at Kristen in the passenger seat. Bernie chose that moment to thrust his nose through the opening between the two front seats, ruining Mike's lame attempt to flirt. He turned into the GCC campus, which was just a few minutes from Kristen's home.

"I've had fun, too," Kristen said, as they unloaded the big dog and began their walk. "You've been open about Anita, and I should return your honesty. It's not just my dad I'm grieving. It's also my former boyfriend. Rob just got married, and it's thrown me more than I expected."

Kristen filled Mike in on the details of her long relationship with Rob, his being enamored with her in black clothing, and their eventual break-up when his attraction to the union secretary became obvious. Mike sensed her underlying feelings of rejection and abandonment but wondered at the stupidity of this Rob person.

"Wow, what a sorry excuse for a man," he said. "I know I'm being harsh about someone I've never met, but I can't imagine why he'd resent your career. He sure left a lot on the table by leaving you."

"Thanks," Kristen said, turning away. "It still stings. When I saw Rob's wedding announcement in the paper, I almost called in sick. Good thing I was testing that day. I didn't have to lecture, just proctor exams. After I put in my office hours, I made a quick getaway for home. Pathetic, huh?"

Mike thought Rob was the pathetic one, but his bedside manner had left him. Instead of mouthing platitudes, he had a sudden urge to hold Kristen, tell her she was beautiful and better off without Rob in her life. Instead, he reached for her free hand. When she didn't pull away, he breathed a sigh of relief.

Look out, fella, he thought. *You're actually being tender to a woman, something Anita always complained you couldn't be with her. Boy, did I wreck my marriage. And now Sophie is paying the price.*

Bernie, with his exquisite sense of timing, took the opportunity to relieve himself. Kristen dealt with the bag and its disposal, and then noted the time. "Mike, it's almost nine. Do you need to get home and prep for tomorrow?"

"I probably should get going," he said. They returned to Kristen's, letting Bernie run in her fenced back yard while they said their goodbyes. "This was a wonderful evening, Kristen. You have no idea how much I've missed home cooking, good conversation, and a family atmosphere. Thank you so much."

And with that little speech, he took her in his arms for a good night kiss. A long, lingering kiss, full of sweetness and not a small amount of passion. Kristen looked startled but didn't back away.

"You're welcome," she said softly. "Have a good day at work tomorrow."

Mike worked the last two days of the current seven-on shift in a more relaxed mood than he'd been in for months. His usual frustration with the GCC nursing students was gone, and he went out of his way to explain his thinking when one timidly asked about a medication dosage on a young, underweight patient.

Annie looked on with a smile. "Dr. Sutliff, I do believe you're adjusting to my class members at last," she said after the GCC undergrads had left. "Before you know it, I'll be letting my first-year students round with you."

"Pushing, pushing," Mike said, grinning. "Annie, I'm doing my best, but let's set some parameters. Could you keep students away on the first day of my shift? I'm covered up and learning all the new patients. Dealing with students is the last thing I need. If you note something that needs my attention, I'll take your feedback, because I know you're a seasoned NP. Would that work?"

"That's actually a great idea," Annie said. "I can use it as a teachable moment, instructing the students about why I questioned you, the rationale I used, and most importantly, how I approached your rattlesnake personality."

Mike laughed loudly, causing staff nearby to look away. *Boy, they are afraid,* he thought. *I've been letting my anger get the best of me.*

At home that night, Mike focused on Kristen. He was free this week, actually for the next seven days, but she would be teaching. He wondered how he could make her week better, as she'd done for him a few nights ago.

With her finely tuned sense of timing, Anita called just as he ready to call Kristen. Instead of maintaining the relaxed state he'd been in, he tensed. What could Anita be upset about now?

"Hi, there," he said. "Anything wrong? Is Sophie alright?"

"Nothing's wrong," Anita said with a huff. "Can't I call to check in after your long work week? How are you doing?"

Mike knew better, but he decided to humor Anita. "Thanks for checking on me," he said. "The week was long, but I've finally adjusted to the schedule. Overall, I'm feeling good about the hospitalist job."

He prayed for patience and continued. "How are you and Grant? Last time we talked, you said he was enjoying his new job."

"He's doing well," Anita said. "I was really calling to ask about something Sophie said today. She mentioned a woman, Christine I think, that you'd been seeing."

As if it's any of your business, Mike steamed to himself. *And I know you well enough that I'm sure you got Kristen's name wrong on purpose.*

"Kristen's her name," Mike said. "You heard me mention her when Sophie got lost at the Fourth of July race, remember?"

"I do now," Anita said. "But I didn't know you two were an item."

"An item? I'm not sure what that means. We've seen each other a few times, and we have a mutual friend from the hospital." *Well, Annie's not technically my friend,* Mike thought. *But Anita's fishing. I'm not going to bite.*

Anita continued to huff. "You know exactly what I mean, Mike Sutliff. I have a right to know if you're seeing someone, and if that someone is a part of my daughter's life. I deserve at least that much heads up."

"Yes, you do," Mike replied, deciding it was better to soothe Anita rather than get involved in an argument about nothing. There were times when Anita just liked to argue. Grant was such an easygoing guy Mike guessed Anita missed the verbal back and forth.

He stayed cool, trying to reassure Anita about Sophie's interactions with Kristen. At the same time, he had to watch out for bruising Anita's ego. She would react like a lioness if she felt threatened by another woman. "Sophie's only been with Kristen a time or two since the race. They got along well, but there was no real bonding."

Now he was fibbing outright. He'd known Sophie liked Kristen a lot when she'd offered to pray when Kristen said she was worried. Kristen seemed to enjoy being with Sophie and was open with her suggestions to get Sophie to eat more. He knew those tips were made out of caring and concern.

"Uh, no," Anita said. "That doesn't fit with what Sophie's saying. She loves Kristen's dog and knows all about Kristen's dad dying. She even asked Grant and me to pray! That's a bond, Mike, whether you want to admit it or not."

"Maybe I missed some things," Mike said, again lying. "But are you opposed to me dating now, Anita? I don't see why you're so upset." Right then he knew he'd bit on the proverbial worm, but he'd had it with Anita's gamey insecurity.

"As always, you've overreacted," Anita said. "I merely wanted to know if there was someone serious in your life. We have our daughter to consider. I'm fine with you dating. I just want to know about the women you introduce Sophie to. Or the one she's praying for!"

"Obviously, you know all there is to know at this point," Mike replied, massaging his temple as a tension headache started to throb. "I'll do a better job in the future of keeping you informed, okay?" *Maybe.*

"Fine, Mike. I didn't want to upset you, but I wanted to clear this up before Sophie comes to your place next weekend. Have a good evening."

After taking two over-the-counter pain relievers, Mike settled in on his sofa to watch an old movie. There would be no sleep for a while. Anita's instincts were usually good; she sensed he and Kristen were more than casual acquaintances. Was she right? What did a good doctor do when there were unanswered questions? It was time to collect more data.

Kristen answered his call on the second ring. "What's up, Mike?" she asked. "Did you make it through your seventy-hour week? I still can't imagine how you do that."

"Made it through with no problems," Mike said. "I'm adjusting to it well. Which is why I called. Now that I'm free for seven whole days, I was wondering about your schedule. Are you flexible this coming week?"

"I'm good in the evenings," Kristen said. "The summer term is about finished, so I'm pushed during the day with grading, writing exams, and seeing students who have realized there's no way they can finish the course without an extension."

"Evenings are fine," Mike said. "You cooked for me, so I want to take you to dinner. How about a steak in Indy?" He realized this was a risk – he was not only asking for a formal date, but for an out-of-town excursion.

"That sounds very nice," Kristen said. "But Friday would be best, since we'll be out late. I can get my rest on Saturday morning. Do I sound like an old lady, or what?"

Mike chuckled. "You sure don't look like an old lady. Not one bit. There's one more thing, though. I'd like to ask a favor, since we're going to be in Indy on Friday."

"What's your favor, Mike?"

Mike gulped. "Would it be possible if we picked up Sophie from her mother's after dinner? She'll be with me for a long weekend, and it will save me a trip on Saturday morning."

The resulting pause made Mike's palms sweat. He hadn't been this nervous since his surgery rotation. He knew he was putting Kristen on the spot. In a big way.

"I guess that's okay," Kristen finally said. "Perhaps we should plan on an early dinner since we'll need to get Sophie at a decent hour."

Mike thanked God for Kristen's tolerance. "Good idea, and you have no idea how much I appreciate your flexibility. Could I pick you up at four on Friday? That gives us an hour to get to Indy, another ninety minutes to eat, and then a half hour to get to Sophie. Would that work?"

"Sure," Kristen said, again without her usual bouncy enthusiasm. "I suppose this means I'll be meeting Anita, right?"

Chapter Five

Kristen ended the call in a funk. What had begun as a promising invitation now felt weird. Mike wanted to take her on a nice date, but they had to pick up Sophie afterward. So much for flirty banter on the way back to Gordon. They'd have a chatty six-year-old in the back seat filling the time. Kristen had to admit she liked Sophie. But Mike was clearly sending a message that any relationship with him included Sophie as part of the package. Which was only right, she supposed. But it still felt funny – they'd barely had a couple of dates, and Mike's message was that going forward, Sophie would be ever present.

The other unspoken part of Mike's message was that Kristen would have to get along with Anita. Or maybe, Kristen would have to be vetted by Anita. Kristen's hackles rose, her rebellious streak gaining strength. What was with this guy? Couldn't he have a few dates without seeking his x-wife's approval?

Or perhaps there was a tricky custody requirement. Maybe Sophie's unconventional schedule with Mike hinged on Anita's final say. Kristen doubted she could ever get seriously involved with a man who had such baggage. Of course, most men her age had a suitcase or two, and so did she. But enough of this convoluted thinking for now! She had to finish her laundry, gather her notes for tomorrow, and get to bed. As she'd told Mike, she was an old lady who needed her sleep.

Kristen arrived at her office early on Monday. She loved her tiny space. Decorated with her handmade crafts, she enjoyed viewing each piece and the memories it held. The floral wreath on the door was her current favorite – summer flowers and butterflies circled a metal frame, topped with a multicolored bow with festive streamers. Once the fall semester started, she would sell the current wreath and replace it with a more seasonal one.

Heather knocked on the door and entered before she could answer. "Dr. Anderson, I wanted to tell you I've spoken to Dr. Stevens about your unfair grading. She's referred me to the dean, which is where I'll go after this. I thought it was only *fair* to let you know."

Kristen took a beat to process Heather's odd announcement. "I appreciate you telling me this in person, Heather. It's certainly your right to protest your grade on the essay question. I wish we'd had a chance to discuss it further last week, but you left before we could."

"I figured there was no point," Heather said. "You practically ridiculed my essay, so why would I want to take more of that?"

"That wasn't my intent at all. I'm sorry if that's how it felt to you. But separate from the test grade, and since you're headed to the dean's office anyway, how are you doing? Is there anything going on at home, or here on campus, that I could help you with? Or maybe someone at the Counseling Center could listen objectively to whatever's bothering you."

"Oh please, don't get all concerned and sweet on me," Heather said, tossing her stringy hair from her face. "And despite all your confidence in the Counseling Center, don't think that I and the other psych majors aren't aware how condescending the faculty members are about students who get therapy. I'm sure you all have our names in a special file, alerting you when we ask for letters of recommendation."

Kristen was so shocked she couldn't reply for a few seconds. "That's not true, any of it. As I've said repeatedly in class, the best counselors are those who have had the experience of being psychotherapy patients themselves. I mean that with all my heart, Heather."

"So I guess you're saying, in your backhanded way, that you've been a patient yourself. Maybe you need to get back 'on the couch.' I don't think you've completed your therapeutic work." With that, Heather turned, stumbled slightly, and left.

Kristen stared at Heather's back as she exited the office. The young woman's malicious tone was new. In the past Heather had been overly confident at times, but never mean-spirited. Her clinical radar was pinging again, though this time it was sending messages about Kristen's vulnerability, not Heather's.

Kristen stewed about the possibilities, both in terms of Heather's distress and her own. Heather could be in a toxic relationship, she could be having parental issues, or she could be experiencing the typical anxiety about grad school and leaving the GCC nest. Kristen wished she could help, but Heather made it obvious that wasn't going to happen.

The dean could make or break Kristen's career. She wondered about his loyalty to Dr. Stevens, and by extension, to her. *I doubt there's much sympathy headed in my direction,* she thought. *If fall enrollments are iffy, a disgruntled student has a lot of power. Way more power than an untenured junior faculty member.*

After grading what seemed to be a mountain of term papers, Kristen decided to call it a day. It was after four, and she was hungry. Time to hang out with Bernie and have a sandwich.

Debra Stevens stood in Kristen's doorway before she had finished gathering her papers for some evening grading. Debra was blunt. "Kristen, I just heard from the dean. I'm to tell you that after the summer term you'll be on adjunct status. He didn't even want to hear your side of the story with regard to Heather's grade. I'm really sorry, but there was nothing I could do." Debra looked upset, and Kristen wondered if Debra's status with the dean was also tenuous.

"That's okay, Debra. I understand you advocated for me the best you could. Do you think it would help if I talked to the dean?"

"He's already said not to bother making an appointment with him," Debra said, her eyes filling. "I've never seen anything like this, Kristen. Try not to personalize it – I heard at the last faculty meeting an untenured chemistry professor had been let go because he'd taken an extra week off with his new baby. He'd cleared it with his department chair, and he was working from home the whole time. None of that mattered."

"That's okay, Debra," Kristen said, realizing she was repeating herself like a robot. "I'll figure things out. Do you know how many courses I'll get in the fall?"

"I'll make sure you get at least two," Debra said. "They'll be the intro courses, though. I'm not supposed to let you teach upper level courses for now."

Kristen smiled and shook her head. "Wow, I've really done a number to my career. But things always work out, usually in unexpected ways, as my father used to say. I'll ramp up my private practice and craft business. Things will work out." There she went, repeating herself again.

"I agree," Debra said. "You'll be fine. And don't discount your teaching ability so quickly, Kristen. I'm glad to write letters of recommendation if you apply to any of the universities in Indianapolis."

"Thanks," Kristen said. "Right now, I'm a little off teaching. Maybe later."

Thinking this was the worst Monday possible, Kristen made sure she drove carefully as she made her way home. If her luck continued, she'd have a flat tire, an oil leak, and get stuck on a railroad track with a locomotive headed her way.

Finally at her house, she bit into her PB&J sandwich, Bernie perched at attention. Her phone jingled. *I've got to change that ring tone,* she thought. *It's much too cheerful for my current mood.* The caller ID indicated it was her mother. *Today just gets better and better.*

"Hi, honey," Kaye chirped. "I wanted to call and reassure you that I'm fine. I've joined a bridge group made up of mostly widows, and I'm seeing things more clearly now. So, instead of talking about me all the time, I want to hear how you're doing."

Kristen considered hiding the truth about her rotten day but didn't have the energy. Being honest would be better. She could gauge how well her mother was doing while venting her own hurt and anger.

"I'm not so good, Mom," Kristen said. "Long story short, I tangled with a student who complained to the dean. As a result, I'll be on adjunct status this fall. My department chair tried to make my case, but she had no luck. I'm not sure what the dean has against me. It must be significant." Holding her breath, Kristen waited to see if her mother would be supportive.

"That's terrible, honey!" Kaye shouted. "What's that dean's name?"

"Mom, you can't call and complain to the dean. I'm a big girl. It wouldn't be appropriate."

"What's his name?" Kaye repeated. "Some dean at GCC asked me out a month after your father died, and I said no, of course. He didn't take it well. He had no awareness that I was grieving. He was also very pretentious about his position."

"His name is Bob Benson. I can't imagine he'd hold your refusal against me after all these months. Mom, that can't be the guy, right?"

"Wrong, honey. Bob Benson was his name. Middling height, gray hair, and tortoise-shell glasses? Dresses kind of pseudo-intellectual, with patches on the elbows of his sport coat? He wears a baseball cap, to add to his appeal to students I'm guessing. He goes for that rumpled but trendy look. Sound right?"

Stunned, Kristen replied. "Yes, that's him, Mom. But I still don't want you calling him, hear me?"

"I won't if you don't want me to. But do you think this would be something to take to human resources? I think this counts as discrimination of some sort, don't you?"

"Maybe. I can't process very well now. But Mom, you have no idea how much your support means to me. I've missed you since you've moved." Kristen admitted to herself she did miss her mother, just not the erratic person she'd turned into after Dad died.

And on the upside, her mother sounded like her old self, smart and willing to defend her daughter at all costs.

"Well, we'll talk this weekend. You can fill me in on any new developments," Kaye said. "What do you have planned for the rest of your week?"

Kristen made a flash decision not to tell her mother about the upcoming date with Mike. Why push her luck? They made small talk for several minutes and ended the conversation with affection. Kristen texted Katie after the call, saying their mother seemed to be doing better.

The rest of the week flew by. Heather was conspicuously absent from class; Kristen assumed she had pulled an A in the course via the dean's intervention. Debra Stevens was nice, but distant. Kristen felt like the department pariah.

Time for lemonade, she thought, remembering her dad's favorite saying during challenging times. *These lemons are getting old.* Kristen's positive outlook gradually returned. She was looking forward to seeing Mike soon.

While she planned her approach to increasing income from crafts, Kristen remembered the Fall Fest would be held in Parke County in October. After a desperate phone call to the craft barn manager, she'd wrangled a last-minute booth, willingly paying the late fee. It made no sense to rely only on holiday shows. She would need more income way before December. Her to-do inventory list included quilted stuffed animals, counted cross stitch Christmas ornaments, decorative birdhouses, wreaths suited to each season, and as a long shot, women's Kentucky Derby hats priced for middle class racing devotees. Derby hats and fascinators went for lots of money, and Kristen could make similar styles for much less. One of her students had told her last semester she and her friends made the yearly trip to Louisville, but they felt dowdy in comparison to the hordes of sophisticated women.

Prior to Mike's arrival, Kristen tallied her inventory list. The investment for raw materials, even if she scored big at summer garage sales, was large. But the potential return looked impressive. She could do this!

The doorbell rang at precisely four. Kristen answered, ready for a night in the big city.

"Hi there!" Mike said, eyeing Kristen's pastel-blue, clingy dress. "You look great, as always."

"Hmmm, as I recall, I looked pretty awful at our first meeting," Kristen said. "Remember my rag-bin top, old shorts, and the dirt smudges from holding Sophie's hand?"

"No one looks good on race day," Mike replied. "You also had extenuating circumstances. You rescued my daughter, for which I'm very grateful."

Eying Mike's snug-fitting beige linen jacket and his chocolate brown slacks, Kristen thought he could be impressive in anything he wore. She wondered how he looked in his hospital scrubs – were they oversized and baggy? Or did his fit, muscular frame fill them out just perfectly? She shook her head when she caught Mike looking at her.

"You okay?" he asked. "You left the room for a minute."

"I'm fine, as I keep telling everyone," she said. Mike remained puzzled but didn't pursue her vague comment. "I'm definitely ravenous for a gourmet steak. Ready to go?" Kristen didn't let him reply, fetching her purse and giving Bernie some good-bye strokes.

"Does Bernie have the run of the house?" Mike asked.

"Yes, he does well on his own. He's quite a Houdini if I try to put him in the crate when I leave. I don't know how, but he always escapes. Then I find him asleep on the couch, giving me an accusing stare when I wake him up. He's even worse when he's boarded. He somehow leaves his carrel and follows staff around as they monitor the dogs."

Mike shook his head. "I was never a big dog person. My mother's allergic, so we had an aquarium."

"If any creature can convert you, it's Bernie," Kristen said firmly. "We're a package deal, just so you know." She eased into Mike's car, closing the door before he could help.

Mike smiled at Kristen. "I understand perfectly. You probably know the same about Sophie and me. I'll admit that after we talked, I wondered about your real response to picking her up after our dinner."

"Sophie isn't an issue," Kristen hedged. "I am a little nervous about meeting Anita. Is her approval part of your package, too?"

"Fair question," Mike said. "Honestly, Anita and I had one of our less productive talks last Sunday. She was upset Sophie was praying for a woman her mom hadn't met." Mike glanced at Kristen as he drove out of town. She looked out the passenger side window for almost a full minute.

"Divorce makes everything so complicated," Kristen said, still avoiding eye contact. What was she supposed to say? Was Mike implying Anita had to give her stamp of approval to Kristen? Suddenly this date was much less fun than she'd hoped. Why did she gravitate to a guy with such a messy combination of male superiority and love for his daughter?

"Complicated is probably a weak descriptor," Mike agreed. "Anita doesn't get to choose my dates, if that's what you're thinking. Yet I can't ignore the fact that she's Sophie's mother." He paused and looked at Kristen again. "Let's change gears. How was your week at GCC?"

"Or we could keep talking about Anita, which would rate about the same in terms of fun conversation," Kristen said. Mike again looked confused, so she knew she owed it to him to be straightforward. "I got demoted this week. After a student protested my evaluation of her essay on a big exam, I was overruled by the dean and put on adjunct status for the fall semester."

Mike seemed shocked but let her continue.

"Actually, once my hurt and anger fizzled out, I began to be excited about doing more with my crafting business. My private practice will also help pay the bills. So, it's 'all good,' as Annie always says. Flexibility is important to me. Adjunct status means I'll set my own hours starting in August."

Kristen looked at Mike as he turned toward the interstate highway. What was he thinking? He'd probably never lost a job in his life. No, he'd been busy being the perfect doctor.

"That's terrible!" Mike reddened, and Kristen noticed he almost missed the entrance ramp. "In med school you took the grade you earned, and no complaining was allowed. We were grateful to be in the program. A poor grade was considered feedback to motivate us to do better. I mean, lives would be at stake if a doctor wasn't trained well. Same in psychology, I would think. Do you have any recourse with this student, or the dean?"

"Not that I know of. My mother, of all people, told me the dean asked her out soon after Dad died. She rebuffed him. She thinks I should go to HR with a grievance. I doubt there's enough to make a case, though. And as I just said, I'm pumped about the freedom in my schedule and the chance to be creative with my crafts."

"It's your call," Mike said, clearly not convinced by Kristen's rationale for accepting the demotion. "If I can help in any way, please tell me. Not sure how that would work, but you never know."

"One thing that comes to mind is allowing me to put flyers advertising my booth at the Fall Fest in the hospital lobby, cafeteria, and gift shop. Do you think the higher-ups would go for that?"

"I'll check first thing when I start back next week," Mike said. "Kristen, I'm really sorry this happened to you. You've got a lot of guts. As a comparison, which you probably don't want, Anita lost a job once and cried for a week. She swore she'd never work for anyone again, and she hasn't. She works from home on a contractual basis as a legal transcriptionist now."

"I'm not a big weeper," Kristen said. "But maybe Anita and I aren't that different. I'm going to work for myself, too."

"Trust me, you and Anita are very different," Mike said with a wink.

His comment helped lighten the mood for the rest of the trip. Mike talked about his childhood, his early interest in medicine, and his joy at being Sophie's dad.

Kristen opened up again about missing her father and told Mike how she and Katie were fierce rivals as kids, fighting constantly. "We never drew blood, but we came close," she said. "It's ironic, now. We're really tight. Since she moved to Phoenix, I've lost a true confidante."

Mike tried not to laugh. "I'm sympathetic, really I am, Kristen. But the thought of you and your sister rolling around on the grass wrestling is hysterical. She must be pretty tough if she came to a draw with you."

"I beg your pardon!" Kristen said with mock anger. "I am a *delicate flower*. Katie fights like a princess, so I won easily every time. But she fought dirty. She was a pincher and a biter!"

Now Mike laughed outright, forgetting his cruise control was on as he approached a semi-truck a little too fast. "We've got to talk about something that lets me focus on the road, Kristen. This highway driving demands more concentration than I've been giving it."

"Fine," she said. "For now, we'll focus on your menu recommendations at the restaurant. What do you like best?"

"The salmon is excellent." Hearing Kristen's unsubtle snort, he added, "But it's a steak house. You can't go wrong with a filet or rib eye. The bone-in cuts are even more tender, but they're very large, usually over a pound. How much of a meat eater are you?"

"After the week I've had, the more meat the better. I'll also want it bloody! I'm in the mood for extra rare. It should moo at me."

"Oh boy," Mike said, shaking his head. "How about some music? I'm thinking light classical."

"I'm thinking Def Leppard," Kristen replied.

Yep, she thought. *It was a raw meat, hard rock kind of evening.*

She'd have to get herself together before she met Anita, or who knew what would happen. Kristen might pinch her, throw her on the lawn, and have at it.

Dinner was a treat. Kristen enjoyed the tender filet topped with butter and grilled shrimp, served on a scalding hot plate. Mike gave in and ordered a rib eye, foregoing his usual fish selection. They laughed over their shared dessert, a six-layer chocolate cake, noting Sophie would be angry if she knew what she'd missed.

The drive to Anita's took about twenty minutes, with Kristen dreading the next portion of the evening. She envisioned Anita as a statuesque former beauty queen and a fiercely protective mother. She was sure Anita blamed Mike for the divorce, and that Grant was a doormat to Anita's overbearing personality.

I need a reality check, she thought. *I haven't even met this woman, and already I'm sure she's a soap opera villain.*

Mike pulled up to a smallish bungalow in Broad Ripple. Similar houses surrounded it. Located one block from the main street, which housed restaurants and a new grocery, the home was both cozy and trendy. Sophie ran out of the house, or tried to, as she lugged her pink suitcase.

"Daddy, I'm all ready," Sophie yelled. Neighbors on the porch next door smiled at the sight of the excited little girl. "Mommy said I should welcome your guest inside. I told her it wasn't a guest, it was just Kristen."

Mike stooped and hugged his daughter. "I've really missed you, honey. As always. Yes, let's go in and say hello to Mommy and Grant."

Giving Kristen the once-over, Sophie said, "You look very nice, Kristen. Your blue dress is almost my favorite color, after pink, which is my Number One."

"Thanks, Sophie," Kristen said with a smile. What was she worried about? Surely a little girl this charming was being raised by two fine parents, not just one.

"Hi, Mike," a female voice said from just inside the front door. "Come on in. Grant's in the back at the grill. And hello, Kristen. I've heard so much about you."

The voice did indeed belong to a beauty. Anita had dark hair similar to Sophie's, but with a touch of auburn. Her eyes were hazel, not icy blue, and her frame petite. Anita was dressed in tight jeans, an old IU T-shirt, and casual sandals. She was gorgeous, but not off-putting.

Mentally crossing her fingers, Kristen extended her hand. "Hi, Anita. It's good to meet you as well. Sophie talks about you all the time. I love your home. Broad Ripple looks like a fun place to live."

"It's good for a small family like ours," Anita said. "Once Sophie is older, we may need to move to a place with better public schools. There's no way we can afford private schools at this point."

Unsure of what Anita was getting at, Kristen stayed quiet. Mike broke in. "Anita, this is Kristen, as you've already figured out. I'm glad you two have met."

Now both women were silent, letting Mike forge on. "How has Sophie been this week, Anita? Has she wandered off? How's her appetite?"

"Hold on, Mike," Anita said. "Let's sit in the living room to talk. Grant is keeping Sophie busy in the back yard, so we can speak freely."

The three gathered in the comfortable room, which was painted a light aqua shade with chocolate-brown, overstuffed furniture. The effect was cozy yet sophisticated.

"To answer your questions, she's been fine, better than in quite a while. We've had fun teaching her the old board games, which she loves. Her attention span is greatly improved. And before she tells on me, I've been giving her more, what should I say, substantive food. She's just too thin, Mike."

Anita tensed, which caused Kristen to wonder. Had Mike been dogmatic about Sophie's food choices? Did he get angry if Sophie was given too many sweets? Was that why Anita had implied Sophie was difficult?

"I agree completely, Anita," Mike said. "I've been experimenting with more options for Sophie, too. I'll be honest and give Kristen some of the credit for that. She also pointed out if I'm too restrictive with Sophie, she'd eventually rebel and eat all kinds of unhealthy things."

Looking at Kristen with new regard, Anita replied. "I'm so relieved, Mike. We've been careful about what we're eating. But everything's not organic or low fat. To be frank, Grant was getting tired of it all. He lost ten pounds, which he didn't need to do."

Grant and Sophie entered the room at that moment, Sophie being carried on his shoulders. Giggling, she announced, "I helped Grant with the food on the grill. I painted the steak with special sauce. I don't have to eat it, but if I did, I'd take at least one bite."

Kristen noted Grant's easy way with Sophie and his lingering glance at his wife. His look spoke volumes – he was devoted to Anita. Kristen was envious.

"Sophie had a grilled cheese, carrot sticks, and a peanut butter cookie before you came," Anita added. "I told her if she was good, you might take her for ice cream when you got to Gordon."

"Sounds like a good plan," Mike said agreeably. Kristen wondered how he was really feeling. Did seeing Sophie giggle with Grant bother him? Was grilled cheese an acceptable sandwich?

"Ice cream always works for me," Kristen said.

"Then let's get going," Mike said. "Sophie's suitcase is in the car. She's accumulated several outfits at my house if we run short. Of course, my mother will buy anything we've forgotten."

"Of *course,* Jane will," Anita said, icicles hanging off her words. "She's one of those grandmas who will spoil a kid rotten if allowed."

Okay, now we're getting down to it, Kristen thought. She noticed Sophie tense slightly as she gripped Grant's shoulders. *Hopefully Mike will stay cool.*

"It's been good to see you two," he said. "Sophie, I'm glad you're eating. A girl with all your energy needs fuel."

As predicted, the girl with all the energy monopolized the conversation for the hour it took to drive back to Gordon. Kristen enjoyed hearing about Sophie's time at her mother's, including extensive descriptions of the board games she had learned to play. Sophie then insisted on hearing everything Bernie had been up to since the DogTrot. Kristen told her eating and sleeping were the highlights of Bernie's typical day, though he would be very glad to see Sophie again.

"I can't wait," Sophie said. "Can we go to your house and eat our ice cream?"

"We'd better eat at the ice cream shop," Mike said. "It's getting a little late for you, so we don't need to make an extra stop at Kristen's."

Kristen knew what he left unsaid. A stop at her house would take at least an hour, given Bernie's pent-up energy and Sophie's delight in seeing him. "Honey, I'm sure you'll see him this week," she said.

"For sure," Mike replied, looking at Kristen. "We'll be seeing Bernie for sure."

After Mike and Sophie dropped Kristen off, she was still combatting emotional fatigue from the situation at work. Meeting Anita and Grant added to her sense of being out of sync. Kristen needed support. Her mother had been sweet, but she needed to talk to a peer. After calling Annie and getting voice mail, she dialed Lauren's number.

"Kristen! I was just thinking about you," Lauren said. "How are things going?"

"Not so good," Kristen admitted. "But before I dump all my junk on you, tell me how you and Bryan are."

"We're just wonderful!" Lauren said. "I was going to tell you in person, but now's as good a time as any. I'm pregnant, due in October. No one knows, because I haven't gained much weight.

My mother was the same way. She didn't show until she was seven months along."

"Alleluia!" Kristen said. "I'm so happy for you. Give Bryan my love as well. This is huge news! What about the rest of your life? How's the new Mohr's doing? I hope it's not adding to your stress during this wonderful time."

Mohr's was formerly the premier local department store, converted a few years ago to a women's boutique specializing in formal and wedding attire. Bryan and Lauren had been instrumental in re-imagining his family's store in an attempt to save it. Between wedding veil kits and a strong online presence, the store had survived.

"Mohr's is also doing well," Lauren said. "We're cautiously optimistic it will be a viable enterprise for a long time. I do have one concern, though. I hope you can help me."

"Name it," Kristen said. "You've been so good to me, what with sharing office space for minimal rent and feeding me patients when your schedule is full. Really, name it."

"It's about my practice, actually. I want to take at least six months of maternity leave, beginning in September. Would you have any time to absorb a few of my long-term patients? Many of them have seen you coming and going from the office, so you're a familiar face. I know I'd be leaving them in good hands, too."

Kristen gulped, which seemed to be her regular reaction lately to good news and bad. She was honored and touched by Lauren's faith in her. "Of course, I'd be glad to," she told Lauren. "In fact, the reason I called was to tell you about my current career woes. You've already solved the bulk of my problems."

Kristen explained the recent developments at GCC, complete with Heather's changed behavior and the dean's odd connection to Kaye. She discussed her plan to increase her craft business, along with reserving booth space at the Fall Fest. As in the past, Lauren was sympathetic, but also logical.

"I agree with your mother," Lauren said firmly. "I'd head right to HR and file a grievance against that idiot dean. You've told me your teaching evaluations have been stellar. You've said they often included written comments, with specific examples of ways you've helped students. Students even wrote about times you made them angry, which they eventually appreciated when they realized you had their best interests in mind."

"Maybe," Kristen said. "I don't want to burn bridges at this point. Perhaps fall enrollments will be better than forecasted and they'll need me full-time."

"Maybe, maybe not," Lauren said. "But I wouldn't count on it. Isn't it wild how each of us has dealt with supervisors who derailed our careers? If Ricky hadn't landed on me, I'd never have gotten into private practice full-time. Now maybe Dean Benson has done you a favor. Your crafts and your patients will keep you plenty busy. You're gifted in both areas, so things will work out."

"That's what I keep hoping".

"Well, they will. God has His eye on us, whether we realize it or not."

"Lauren, your faith has always boosted you. I just can't think like that."

"You just can't think like that *yet*," Lauren said. "It will come, I know it. I've been praying for you."

The two women then planned how the transfer of Lauren's patients would occur, with Kristen assuming what amounted to a full-time caseload by early September. Kristen told Lauren she would need ten days off for the Fall Fest. Lauren was sure clients would be fine with that, if given enough advance notice.

"You might have a few patients who show up to buy your wares," Lauren added. "You'll have to think about how to handle it. It shouldn't be a problem as long as you treat them like every other customer. No special discounts, no bartering for their next session. Makes sense, right?"

Kristen was again thankful for Lauren's experience and wisdom. Too bad she hadn't had Lauren with her when Heather had pitched her angry fit. Kristen had been so blindsided she wasn't able to react.

She'd have to think about Lauren's input concerning HR. Did she want to rock the boat that much? Would it matter?

Saturday was hot and muggy, a perfect day to plow through some craft items while staying indoors in the air conditioning. Kristen enjoyed running and other outdoor activities, but a heat index of over a hundred degrees with high humidity was just plain dangerous. Even Bernie was content to stay inside and watch her work.

Several hours later, Kristen realized she hadn't had lunch. What she did have, she thought proudly, were ten items ready for sale. She'd worked on a random sampling from her inventory list but became aware she needed to have an organized focus, perhaps an assembly line type plan, to increase her output. Ten items would sell in about as many minutes. Munching on her ham sandwich, she heard the doorbell ring.

"Kristen, it's me-e-e," Sophie chanted. "Daddy and I are here to take you to the movies."

Opening the door, Kristen saw Sophie and Mike, each carrying a packet of candy. Bernie tried to take Sophie's candy, but she moved away from his leap just in time. Kristen couldn't resist commenting. "Candy for the movies, huh? That's a good plan – a special treat, but not something that happens every day."

Mike grinned sheepishly. "The label says they're made from real fruit juice," he said. "Sophie convinced me they were almost a food group. Like your apple crisp, remember?"

Sophie ran into the house, stopping short when she saw Kristen's craft table. Wreaths, stuffed animals, and a few random Christmas items covered the surface. "Oh, I want to learn to do this stuff," Sophie cooed. "Everything is so pretty. What's this, a gun? Are you going to sell guns, too?"

"No, honey, that's a glue gun," Kristen explained. "You can't use a tool like that on your own. I'm very careful, but I still get burned sometimes." Kristen held out her left hand, showing Sophie a few old blisters.

"Ouch!" Sophie said, stepping back. "I'll learn to do something else." She sat by Bernie, who instantly rolled on his back for a stomach rub.

"What's this about the movies?" Kristen asked.

"We weren't presuming you'd have nothing else planned, honestly," Mike said. "But Sophie's been wanting to see the newest full-length animated feature. We thought we'd see what you were up to in case you wanted to come."

"Sorry," Kristen said. "I've budgeted all of today's free time for craft production. It's important I build my inventory for my booth at the Fall Fest. They frown on vendors who sell out early and leave an empty space."

Sophie began to pout but caught herself. "I understand, Kristen. Maybe we could do something tomorrow."

Kristen and Mike looked at Sophie, then at each other. Clearly Sophie was improving behaviorally and emotionally. Each smiled, understanding Sophie's comment meant she was more able to defer fun and empathize with others.

"I really appreciate you understanding," Kristen said, kneeling down to Sophie's level. "Tomorrow is a good idea. What could we do then?"

"What do you want to do, Daddy?" Sophie asked, looking at Mike. "You should get to choose since I chose the movie today."

"We're free after church," he said. "No plans other than that."

Kristen had a thought. "I'd planned to spend tomorrow crafting, too, like today. But I'll need to eat. How about if you two come by after church? I'll serve brunch. Sophie, you may have to try some new foods, but I guarantee there will be some you'll love."

Chapter Six

As he left Kristen's with Sophie in tow, Mike thought about her refusal to go to spend the afternoon with them. Was Kristen trying to distance herself? Did meeting Anita cause her to rethink his complex family situation? Would she end their budding relationship after just a few encounters because of Anita and Grant?

No, she wouldn't. Mike was sure Kristen had more strength than that. Maybe it was just as she'd said – she had to build her inventory of crafts and she was on a roll, not to be interrupted for a movie at a minute's notice. Anyway, she'd offered to cook them brunch. He'd thought about asking her to go to church with them, but it was too soon. And as he recalled, she didn't have lots of positive things to say about faith.

Sophie broke into his thoughts. "Daddy, wasn't Bernie good today? He didn't mess with Kristen's craft table, and he let me pet him. He didn't jump much either. Don't you think a good dog like Bernie would be great for us to have?"

"No, I don't," Mike said gently. "I work long days when you're not in town. That wouldn't be fair to a dog. He or she would be very lonely."

"Well, Mommy can't get a dog because Grant doesn't like them," Sophie said. "I guess I'll have to make do with Bernie and pretend he's mine."

Great. He'd found another way to disappoint Sophie. The divorce still hurt, mostly at times like this, when his daughter poignantly referred to her sense of loss without realizing it. Why couldn't Anita have given him another chance? Had he really wanted one? He'd exited the marriage as if it were another task on his master list. He'd been a fool.

After the film, he and Sophie had a simple supper, then before her bedtime she continued her campaign for a dog.

"I need to pray, Daddy," she said. "Dear Jesus, thank you for this pretty day. Thank you for Mommy, Daddy, and Grant. Thank you for good friends like Kristen and Bernie. Help us figure out how to have a dog with Daddy's long work schedule. Amen."

"Amen," Mike said, kissing Sophie on the forehead. "Sleep tight, little one. I love you."

Unable to focus on reading his usual action thriller, Mike channel-surfed in vain for something to watch. Nothing appealed. Rom-coms were not to his taste, tonight especially. They never addressed the craziness of real-life. Everything was tied up in a bow after ninety minutes. On-demand movies were violent and depressing. He sighed and grabbed the Bible on his coffee table. *When in doubt*, he thought, *turn to the Lord.*

And as always, God didn't disappoint. Verses about trusting God, having faith that bad times would pass, and praising the Lord in all your circumstances leapt out at Mike. He even turned to Proverbs 31 and read about the ideal Godly woman. He had to admit both Anita and Kristen fit many of the descriptions. Both were hard working, loyal, and faith-filled. Kristen denied having faith, but he knew her sense of hope and optimistic nature had to come from God. He just needed to remind her of that.

Oh boy, now I'm evangelizing the woman I'm dating. Was he being presumptuous? Would she be alienated if he referred to God too much? Probably, but it was who he was. She might as well know that about him. Before it got more serious.

Sunday morning was hot again, with a brutal heat index and oppressive humidity typical of late summer in Indiana. Mike and Sophie were glad to get into Kristen's air-conditioned house after the close quarters at church. The scent of home cooking filled the air.

"Yum! It smells good in here," Sophie announced. "What are we having, Kristen?"

Mike broke in. "Sophie, we talked about this. We're supposed to come in and thank Kristen for having us. And give her this." Mike held out a potted plant full of Black-Eyed Susans. "The petals reminded us of your hair," he said.

"You didn't have to bring anything, but I love them," Kristen said as she wiped her hands on her dish towel. "To answer your question, Miss Sophie, here's our menu. Breakfast burritos with eggs, avocado, and black beans. Fresh fruit with honey/yogurt dressing. Finally, whole grain waffles. What do you think?"

"I think I'll try a bite of each," Sophie said, clearly not sure of the exotic menu Kristen described.

"That's great, sweetie," Mike said. Looking at Kristen, he continued. "This all sounds like a lot of work. You didn't have to cook so much for us."

"Actually, it was all pretty easy. And I cheated on the waffles. I bought the freezer kind, so Sophie could help by making them."

"I love to help! And I see the stool I can stand on by the toaster. But where's Bernie?"

"He's at his play group," Kristen said. "He usually goes on Saturdays, but yesterday he was so good while I worked, I let him stay home. I took him today so we could eat in peace."

"Oh." Sophie said, looking down at Bernie's food bowl. "Maybe we could go get him after we eat."

"I've paid for the day, so I won't pick him up until later this afternoon," Kristen explained. "I was going to work on my crafts after brunch. It would be too much to expect Bernie to be good two days in a row."

Brunch commenced, with Sophie trying each item on the menu. She pronounced the burritos too spicy for her taste. The fruit salad was a hit, but the waffles were the clear winner.

"These are very delicious, and I helped make them," she said. "The syrup is also very good."

Mike laughed. "I think you have more syrup than waffle on your plate, Sophie. But that's fine – you tried everything. I'm proud of you."

Looking at Kristen, he smiled and continued. "Thanks for the fine meal. We usually have cereal and toast after church. This was very fancy."

"Very fancy," Sophie echoed, her face smeared with waffle goo. "We'll have to cook for you sometime, Kristen."

Mike started to protest, and then caught himself. Why not? He could cook a little. Well, he could grill and buy sides at the store. He'd have to avoid his usual total veggie menu, but Kristen would eat chicken, he knew. As he was about to ask her for dinner some evening this week, his pager went off. His cell phone dinged a few beats later, so he knew it was the hospital forwarding the message. He left to make the call, returning with a frown.

"What's up, Mike?" Kristen asked. "Anything wrong?"

"Nothing big, just the usual health care job demands. The hospitalist covering this week had a family emergency. They need me to come in for the rest of today and all of tomorrow. The wrinkle is my parents are out of town visiting my aunt in Lexington. I need to start calling sitters."

Kristen looked at Sophie. Sophie looked at Kristen, mouthing, "Please, please, please."

"Sophie could stay here until you get off at seven," Kristen said. "I've got plenty of food. We'll break up the afternoon when we get Bernie, and if she gets tired, I'm sure she'll take a little nap for me."

"I will, I will," Sophie said. "I'll help you, too. Bernie and I can play while you make stuff."

Kristen hesitated, and then added, "And Sophie is welcome tomorrow, too. If you bring her by on your way to work, she and I can have breakfast together. I don't have any classes, so I'm free."

Mike's brain was working hard. Kristen's offer would solve

a myriad of problems. His usual back-up sitters were less than impressive. They watched several children during the summer months. Since Sophie wasn't a regular, she often felt left out, and was sometimes teased by the older children. More importantly, he would see how Kristen and Sophie got along for several hours, not just for the occasional meal or picnic. This was Kristen's chance to be a real Proverbs woman.

Could I be more condescending? he asked himself. *No wonder Anita called me out for that so often. Here I am testing Kristen instead of being grateful. Forgive me, Lord.*

"Kristen, that's hugely generous of you," he said. "I'll pay you the going rate. But it would help both Sophie and me if she could stay with you."

"You will not pay me," Kristen said with a shrug. "I'm doing this for two friends, thank you very much."

"No offense intended," Mike replied. "I didn't mean to insult you."

"He's that way sometimes," Sophie said. "Mommy says to ignore it."

Kristen laughed, and Mike was relieved. He had to get moving, though. Time to get his work game going.

At the hospital Mike immersed himself in the tasks left on the patient list. The other physician had rounded on almost everyone, but his notes were sketchy, done in a code known only to him. Mike stopped by the rooms of newly admitted patients, introducing himself and apologizing for the confusion in coverage. Patients were generally fine with his explanation. Some were even relieved; Mike had heard his counterpart could be lacking in compassionate bedside manner. Since it was Sunday he didn't have to deal with medical or nursing students. Tomorrow would be a different story.

After a quick cafeteria supper, he relaxed in the team room to enter his notes into the computer. He forced himself to focus; his thoughts seemed to return to Kristen no matter what he was typing.

She had really stepped up to help him and Sophie. She stepped up, in fact, at a time when her life was in chaos, when she needed time at home to build inventory. He'd figure out a way to repay her, to help her somehow. He'd even buy lots of items at her festival table. He doubted they would go with his minimalist décor, but Sophie would have fun putting stuffed animals and wreaths all over her room at his place.

His shift ended, finally. Driving over to Kristen's, he wondered how the day had gone. It hadn't been a full day, though. Noon to seven was a tolerable time to deal with Sophie; tomorrow would be the real test. Twelve-plus hours with Sophie Sutliff could challenge even the best of caregivers.

Kristen met him at the door before he could ring the bell. "Sophie and the 'best dog in the world' are asleep on my bed," she said. "Bernie is always tired after his play group. I think that gave Sophie permission to nap, too."

Mike smiled, fixing his gaze on Kristen as they both entered her living room. "Again, thank you so much," he said. "I don't think you realize what a lifesaver you are."

He turned her gently toward him, cupped her face in his hands and kissed her firmly. Her lips responded to his, and he could smell that subtle perfume she always wore. She looked shocked, but then smiled. He took that as a good sign and kissed her a second time, noting that her curls tickled his chin. After a few seconds, Kristen's arms reached around his neck, threading through his hair.

"My, Dr. Sutliff, that was quite a kiss," she finally said, flustered and looking away. "Are you sure about this? I'm happy to watch Sophie when you're in a bind, but there seems to be more going on here."

"I'm pretty sure there's a lot more going on," he said. "Kristen, you're a wonderful woman, one I'd like to get to know much better. Separate from Sophie's obvious love of you and Bernie, I'd like to see you more often. I'm a guarded guy, as you probably know. But you've touched something in me."

What a dumb speech, he thought. He might as well be writing high school poetry. Kristen did touch something in him, but he sure wasn't smooth about letting her know.

"I like you, too," Kristen said. "We'll have to be careful, though. I don't want Sophie to get hurt if something changes between us."

What did that mean? Was she backing off, or rejecting him in a kind way? Maybe she was sincere. Sophie had to be considered if there were to be a relationship between them. That was good, right? She was showing some feelings for both him and his daughter. He decided to be positive and go with her surface message, not the paranoid ones he was generating.

Well, there's just one thing to do, he thought, grinning at Kristen. He kissed her again. Most importantly, she responded again, pressing her body into his. *Maybe women liked this high school stuff.*

They heard a bark, a jingle from collar tags, and footsteps padding down Kristen's hallway. Kristen and Mike separated before Sophie appeared, her hair mussed, with Bernie by her side. "Daddy, you smell like soapy bleach. How was work?"

"It was fine," he said, picking his precious girl up. "Are you ready to come home? We have to get your things collected for tomorrow."

"I don't need much," Sophie said, now completely awake. "Since I'll be here, I don't have to pack lunch, snacks, or my nap pillow. Right, Kristen?"

"Right," Kristen said. "It might be a good idea to pack a change of clothes, in case Bernie gets you messy. Other than that, I've got what we need."

Mike was struck by his daughter's matter-of-fact statement about the reality of day care. Even though his parents watched her most of the time, she spent plenty of time in child care settings, either in Gordon or Indy. Which was okay, just not the same as being home. Or with someone, like Kristen, who cared about you more than paid staff might. And who might just care about him as well.

At a few minutes before seven the next day Mike dropped Sophie off at Kristen's. They seemed happy to see each other. Kristen told Sophie there were egg sandwiches for breakfast, along with orange juice and milk. As Mike left, Kristen handed him an egg sandwich in a baggie.

"For your breakfast," she said. "I have a feeling you're functioning on black coffee at present, despite your devotion to quality nutrition."

"Good call," Mike said. "This looks great. Chances are it will be gone by the time I pull into the parking lot at Gordon Memorial."

"Have a good day," Kristen said.

"Yes, Daddy, have a good day," Sophie called out, arms around Bernie's neck. "Heal all the sick people."

He swallowed hard as he drove to the hospital. He hadn't realized how much he missed being part of a real family, even if Kristen was nowhere near being his partner. Mike floated into work, a full stomach and good attitude accompanying him. He checked in at the team room, got his patient list for the day, and began rounds. As he'd predicted yesterday, medical and nursing students made the rounding team huge. The group filled the hallway, edging into patient rooms at times.

"Hi, Dr. Sutliff," Annie said. "Per our agreement, my students are going to observe rounds today, and keep their questions to themselves. Is that still okay with you?"

"Perfect," Mike said. "Looks like the hospital is full. I haven't seen all the beds occupied in quite a while."

"Yep, there's chatter that the eastside Indy hospital is funneling admissions to us while they remodel. I feel for the families of the patients. It's quite a drive to get here when they're already stressed."

"Thanks, Annie. I'll remember that as I round. Families are as important to the healing process as our services," Mike replied.

Annie looked at him in shock. Obviously, she was wondering where grumpy Dr. Sutliff had gone. He caught her gaze before she could look away. After a hearty laugh, he said, "Annie, I can tell you're surprised. It's all due to you. Your pointed comments about my attitude were right on target. I listened closely, despite what you may have thought."

After another pointed look, Annie replied. "I doubt it's my input, Dr. Sutliff. I think I've got to give Kristen a call tonight. She called on Friday, but I wasn't available. It's obvious she and I need to talk."

Rounds were smooth, which was unusual for a Monday. Patients presented with everything from heart problems, to infected wounds, to simple post-partum care. Mike was conscious to pick up on family stressors, especially regarding struggles getting to Gordon from Indianapolis. Annie was again impressed.

"My, my, your bedside manner has really taken off, Dr. Sutliff," she said when the students had dispersed. "What's the big change, if it wasn't my excellent guidance?"

Realizing Annie knew perfectly well why he was in such a good mood, he took a risk. Mike hated gossip, but he wanted to let Annie know he cared for Kristen. "You were right when you said you needed to call Kristen. She's great, isn't she?"

"Uh huh. She is." Annie's eyes darkened and her tone was fierce. "If you hurt her, Dr. Sutliff, there will be serious consequences. And I'm not just talking about setting my students free during rounds. Kristen is the best woman I know. She deserves the best man around. Make sure you're up to that. Nurses hold a lot of power in hospitals, and I'll sic them on you if Kristen suffers."

Mike watched as Annie charged down the hall. Kristen sure inspired loyalty in her friend. He'd better be up to the challenge.

After his long day, Mike was looking forward to having the rest of the week off. He and Sophie had made a "fun to-do list" for the week, and they would have to check it tonight to plan tomorrow's activities. He rang Kristen's bell, opening the door when he heard a chorus of "Come in" and a loud bark.

He was shocked at what he saw next. Perched on a chair at Kristen's dining room table, Sophie was holding a glue gun, carefully attaching flowers to a small decorative wreath. The wreath already had miniature unicorns placed around the frame. How could Kristen be so careless with his little girl?

"Are you kidding me?" he shouted as he rushed to his daughter. "Sophie shouldn't be using a glue gun. Kristen, you've got the blisters to prove it. Sophie, are you okay?"

Kristen and Sophie looked at him as if he were green. Bernie growled and stood, picking up on his anger.

"Mike, settle down," Kristen said. "Sophie is using a cold melt glue gun. I would never let her use my hot glue gun. Give me some credit, will you?" She breathed hard, staring at him with narrowed eyes.

Mike had never seen Kristen angry. She, unlike Sophie's glue gun, was white hot. He kind of liked the look – fiery and passionate – but unfortunately it was for all the wrong reasons.

"My bad," he said weakly. "I jumped to conclusions, and I was concerned for Sophie's safety. I should have known better."

"Yes, you should have, Daddy," Sophie scolded. Looking at Kristen, she continued. "Mommy says Daddy always thinks the worst. And he doesn't let people explain themselves."

"Whatever," Kristen said. "I get where your Mommy's coming from. Anyway, gather your things together, Sophie. I'll finish this wreath and have it for you when I see you next. I'm not sure when that will be, though." She ignored Mike and bent over the dining table to organize the unfinished projects. Bernie growled again.

Now he had to make amends to Kristen *and* Bernie. And he had to do it before Annie called. "Look, I'm tired," he said. "I thought Sophie was using a hazardous tool. I should have known you would never put Sophie in any kind of danger. You're too smart and caring to ever do such a thing."

"I am," Kristen said. "Too bad you don't know that yet. Enjoy the rest of your week with Sophie. She's talked nonstop about all the fun things you've got planned." She turned to fetch Sophie, who was lugging her backpack.

"And I didn't even need to change my clothes, Daddy. That's

why my backpack is full," she said. "I was very neat and careful today."

"You were great, honey," he said. "But if you were messy, that would be okay too."

They made their way to the front door. Mike turned to say goodbye to Kristen, and found the door closing in his face. Making amends hadn't worked. At all. The drive home was silent until Sophie weighed in.

"You hurt Kristen's feelings," Sophie said. "She told me when people are angry it means there's another feeling under it, like hurt or being scared. She was sure angry, huh?"

"For sure," Mike said.

After listening to Sophie's prayers and tucking her in, Mike gathered his thoughts. His outburst at Kristen was an honest mistake. He loved Sophie so much, and he'd heard Kristen talk about her glue gun burns more than once. Kristen would forgive him, right? He tapped her number into his phone, only to be greeted by the "leave a message" recording. Obviously, Kristen was talking to Annie and couldn't be bothered to interrupt that call for his. He was still in big trouble.

On Tuesday he and Sophie began to whittle down their fun list. They went to the city park, enjoying the water slide and playground. Mike was struck by Sophie's athleticism, and by the fact that she knew how to swim. Anita hadn't told him about that. Maybe part of Sophie's hyper nature was the lack of physical activity. She spent a lot of time sitting – in school, in the car, and at Anita and Grant's when they were tired after their workdays. He'd have to figure out how to keep Sophie more active.

A trip to the grocery followed, with Mike allowing Sophie to pick one item of her choice for every two he put in the cart. For the most part she chose foods with good nutritional quality – fresh fruit, cheese sticks, and pretzels. He let the chocolate bars enter the cart as well. Kristen had said if given the chance, Sophie would choose mostly healthy foods with the occasional treat. As usual, Kristen was right.

After putting things away at his house, Sophie chose dinner. They were munching on cheese pizza when she began her questioning.

"Daddy, have you called Kristen yet? Did you tell her you were sorry for yelling at her?"

"I didn't yell, did I?" he asked, sure that he hadn't.

"You did, Daddy. Remember I said you hurt her feelings? You hurt my feelings, too."

Sophie looked at him with anxious eyes, probably worried he would become angry again. What a mess he'd made.

"I'm sorry, Sophie. I sure didn't mean to hurt you. I love you more than anything. I tried to call Kristen last night, but she was busy."

"Maybe it's like when you and Grandma talked to me about asking a grown-up for help when I looked for you at the race. Maybe you need to think first, like you told me. Then your temper wouldn't come out." Again, Sophie looked concerned, waiting to see how he would take her words.

Mike looked at his daughter in wonder. Such wisdom. From the mouths of babes, or so he'd heard. "You're absolutely right, Sophie. I need to think before I get mad. Your mom said that a few times, didn't she?"

Clearly relieved, Sophie smiled. "Mommy knows a lot. But so do you, Daddy. You're the best doctor in the whole wide world. If you want, I'll help you think before you get mad."

"Thanks, honey. That would be good," Mike said.

"So, have you called Kristen today? I think you should, and when she talks you should listen to her. I'll help you think before you speak," Sophie said quietly.

"Let's try now," he said. Tapping her number, he was connected to voice mail for the second time in as many calls. Sophie nodded, insistent that he leave a message.

"Hi, Kristen. It's Mike. I wanted to call and apologize again for my anger last night. You were an angel to watch Sophie, and she had a great time with you. Please give me a call when you can." Sophie gave him the "keep going" sign, so he continued. "I know you're busy winding up the summer term and building your inventory. You're such a giving person. I forgot how much you sacrificed to watch Sophie for two days. Please know I appreciate you more than you realize." Getting no further direction from Sophie, he ended the call.

Sophie blew out what seemed to be high volumes of compressed air from holding her breath. "That was pretty good, Daddy. We'll see if she calls. But don't give up."

"I won't, honey. I won't."

With Sophie tucked in and asleep, Mike did his usual nightly ritual of channel surfing and attempting to read. He was about to listen to some soft jazz when his phone's ring tone played. *Sophie's not here to help this time,* he thought when he saw the caller ID. *Give me wisdom, Lord.*

"Hi Kristen," he said. "Thanks so much for calling me back. How was your day?" Dumb, dumb, dumb. He was trying to make small talk when he should have been groveling.

"It was fine," Kristen said, after a pause. "I tied up my final grading for the summer term. I cleared out my personal things from the office, since I'll be an adjunct in a month. Adjunct faculty members don't usually have their own offices. Then I came home and worked on my inventory for the festival. No burns today."

No burns. Only the one she was giving him. Deservedly so.

"That's a big day. I can imagine it was draining on many levels. You deserve better, Kristen. From GCC, and from me. I apologize to you a lot, but I'm learning a new way to deal with things. I hope you can forgive me for yelling at you. I didn't even realize I did, but Sophie told me." Mike waited, wondering what Kristen was thinking.

"Yes, you yelled," she said. "It made me think I don't really know you. I know Sophie, and she's a part of you, but that's not the same."

"No, it's not. That's why I want us to see each other more, without Sophie," he said, almost pleading.

"Maybe," Kristen responded, caution in her voice. "This week and next are bad for me, with building my stock for the Fall Fest and prepping for the two intro courses. I haven't taught them in a while, so I need to make fresh notes and computer links. I also have to meet with Lauren for a few afternoons, to review the cases I'm going to absorb when she goes on maternity leave. I'll give you a call when things settle down, okay?"

"Sure, I'll be looking forward to hearing from you," Mike said. With that, Kristen ended the call. He'd been dismissed. Memory flashes surged through his brain. This feeling was very familiar. Anita had confronted him time and again about his abrupt manner, his arrogant responses to her concerns, and of course, his temper. He'd never gotten physical, but when he was mad everyone knew it. He realized the divorce hadn't been only about his long work hours. It was about him.

Chapter Seven

Kristen felt like a fool. She'd been filled with gushing dreams about Mike's kisses, his love for Sophie, and the possibility the three of them could one day be a family. Anita and Grant seemed like good people, and Kristen had envisioned all of them co-parenting Sophie together. Mike was wonderful - romantic, generous, and hard working. Until something set him off, and until he judged others against some impossible standard.

When Annie had called last night, they spent a little time catching up. The majority of the conversation, though, centered on Mike's angry flare when he saw Sophie with the glue gun. He'd been so quick to assume Kristen was careless, even cavalier, with his daughter's safety. The only positive thing from the event was that Sophie hadn't seemed to be upset or scared of her father. Kristen hoped that was a good sign. Annie listened like the good friend she was, and then broke in.

"There's more here than you being insulted. Kristen, what's really up?"

"That's it. I'm telling you, Mike was a real bear, almost frightening, when he saw Sophie with the cold melt glue gun. It was demeaning to me. And to be that way in front of a six-year-old! I can't imagine what you've gone through at the hospital with him." Kristen was on a roll, intent on convincing Annie that Mike was an ogre.

"Yes, he's been tough. But lately, he's been much better. In fact, I'd attributed that to you. I could tell Sophie was crazy about you, and that he liked you. I figured you two had been seeing each other since that time at the fireworks." Annie waited for Kristen to reply.

"We have seen each other," Kristen admitted. "I've met the x-wife and her husband. I've cooked Mike and Sophie brunch. He's kissed me a few times. No big deal."

"Yeah, no biggie then," Annie drawled, full of sarcasm. "I'm getting the picture now. You've been busy with more than work. Here I thought the ruckus with the entitled student, making crafts, and dealing with Lauren's clients were the reasons for your lack of contact. But those are minor things. Don't you get it Kristen? You don't ever give your heart freely. You were trusting Mike, and he's let you down. Right?"

"My heart is fine," Kristen said. "I just hurt for Sophie. I'll miss her, too."

"What? What do you mean, 'you'll miss her?' Are you thinking of breaking it off with Mike without having a real fight? Without confronting how he acted, and how he hurt you? Good grief, have you forgotten what happened when you didn't call out Rob on all of his baloney?"

"That was different," Kristen said. "Rob was interested in the woman at the office. I was on top of that."

"Yes, after he told you how to dress, challenged how much you loved your work, blah, blah, blah. You're a real tough one." Annie's continued sarcasm was unusual for her. Kristen took note.

"You may have a tiny point. But don't you think I have enough to deal with right now without having to handle a diva physician? I've got to make some money. I can't keep babysitting for free and getting all gaga over some guy."

"He didn't offer to pay you?" Annie demanded. "I can't believe that."

"Well, he did offer," Kristen conceded. "I refused. Sophie's a joy. And Bernie actually did a lot of the babysitting for me. They were inseparable."

"You have some difficult thinking to do," Annie said. "I can't believe I'm being the voice of reason here. I sound like you when you're in your psych mode. What do you want from your life? The clock is ticking, girl. Mike's a catch, and his daughter is a sweetie. Time for you to decide what's important to you. More to the point, it's time to be a big girl and stand up for yourself."

Still tired after a fitful night's sleep, Kristen needed to work off some tense energy. As usual, she focused on her crafts. A quick inventory revealed a stash of over fifty items, with varying price points. She needed more prior to the festival in October. Lots more.

Setting up an assembly line to make stuffed bears, she began. Using a rotary cutter for the simple shapes allowed her to cut several thicknesses of fabric at once. A self-healing cutting mat, certainly one of the wonders of the modern world, protected her dining table. By sewing all of one bear body part at each stage, she was able to put together six bears in the time it used to take her for one or two. It was work, though. By lunchtime she was both famished and tired. It was time for food and a change of craft scenery.

One quick deli chicken sandwich later, Kristen thought about her next project. Since the cutter and table mat were already out, she stuck with fabric projects. A midsummer sale at the fabric store had resulted in several yards of holiday fabric. Time for placemats and napkins.

Cutting the straight lines was much easier than the bear body parts. By late afternoon she had several sets of holiday linens ready to sell. Kristen mused about how to make them special. Surely there would be gazillions of holiday table items at the festival. What would make hers stand out?

Searching through her collection of holiday magazines took another hour, but with good results. She had several options. She could embroider tiny Christmas trees on the corner of each mat, but that would take too much time. She could pair each mat and napkin with a holiday mug, which she'd noticed for sale at the dollar store. Or she might go big and sell sets of four mats and napkins along with a matching full table service for four. The dollar store had advertised plates, mugs, and bowls in coordinating holiday patterns. When paired with her set of linens, the effect would be charming.

It would also look like it cost a lot more than I spent, she thought. *I could charge enough to cover my labor and materials costs and still make a good profit.*

By seven, she'd added significantly to her inventory. She was starved. A quick cheese omelet, along with an almost overripe banana, served as supper. Kristen was satisfied. It was time to relax after a productive day.

As she tried to focus on the latest binge-watch recommendation from her students, her mind wandered. Was Annie right that Mike was a catch? Was she reading too much into one lapse of temper, one that was prompted by his love for Sophie? Kristen hated conflict, which was one of her weaknesses as a therapist. Despite her fights with Katie, their disputes were routine sibling tussles. She hadn't grown up in an angry home, so she couldn't figure out why she avoided differences of opinion. Maybe that *was* why; by never having much experience with anger, she didn't know how to deal with it except to avoid it. Deep Freudian analysis would probably yield the cause of this defect, but she didn't have the time or the money for that. She just needed to grow up a little. Or a lot.

She debated calling Mike. Not yet. She'd told him she had a busy two weeks ahead, which was true. Contact with him might derail her focus on other tasks. Her cell phone pinged with a text from Lauren, asking her to call if it was convenient. Kristen called immediately.

"Hey, Preggers! How are you doing?" Kristen asked. "I was going to call you later this week."

"I think I'm okay, but the baby may be coming sooner than we thought," Lauren said. "I'm on bed rest for my blood pressure, so I can't see my patients starting *immediately*. We need to strategize about you stepping in a little sooner than we'd planned."

"Whatever you need," Kristen said, cold beads of sweat beginning to form on her forehead. "Is the baby going to be born soon? Are you going to be all right?

"I'll be fine," Lauren said with true confidence. "God is with me, and with our little boy. Bryan is a bit of a mess, but he'll be fine, too."

Lauren's faith had always been a source of wonder and envy to Kristen. She was grateful for her friend's belief now, though. "You're absolutely right, Lauren," she said. "It will all be fine. Your doctors are excellent, and obviously they're on top of things. What's our next step?"

Lauren hesitated. "I'm sorry to dump this on you so soon, but ethically I need to cover my patients. Could you come over tomorrow? We could review the people who want to continue with you, and maybe even schedule some of the more crucial folks for Friday. I'm asking a lot, but I need you, Kristen."

Still clammy, but touched by Lauren's confidence in her, Kristen replied instantly. "You've been there for me plenty of times, my friend. What time should I be there tomorrow?"

After ending the call with an appointment at Lauren's bedside for ten in the morning, Kristen thought about the unpredictability of life. Lauren was a healthy young woman, so how could she have high blood pressure? Yet she was calm as she discussed what needed to be done for Kristen to assume care of her clients. *I wish I had some of that confidence, that peace.*

She remembered Mike was a person of faith also. He had a temper, but then everyone was human. Aside from that, he was a good person, a wonderful father, and a caring doctor. His divorce continued to bother her, though. What could have happened that was so impossible to reconcile? Had Anita just wanted out? Why did Mike give up on his marriage after finishing his medical training? Kristen wished she knew. More importantly, she had to have the guts to find out.

Kristen pulled into Lauren's drive just before ten on Thursday morning. She brought muffins and a casserole, thinking Bryan could use both the food and the support. A call of "Come on in," answered her knock on the door.

"I'm in the bedroom, of course," Lauren said. "Bryan left for the store, knowing you were on your way."

"It's so good to see you," Kristen said as she gave Lauren an awkward hug, standing over her good friend's bedside. She was startled by Lauren's appearance; she was smiling but her face and lips were distinctly rounded. Her hands and fingers were also swollen, adding to the fear in Kristen's heart.

"I know I look like a puffer fish," Lauren said. "My doctor wants to see me again tomorrow. If my blood pressure hasn't gone down, they'll admit me to Gordon Memorial. But it will all be fine." Despite the courage in Lauren's words, Kristen caught the anxiety in her eyes.

"If they can't stabilize you, what will happen? I mean if they induce you, how early will that make Baby Dawson?"

"Six weeks," Lauren said. "It's scary, for sure. Hopefully they'll be able to normalize my blood pressure in the hospital. If he's induced early, they're saying the baby may need to be transported to the Riley NICU in Indianapolis. Bryan's beside himself, and our parents aren't much better. God is with us, though, of that I'm sure."

Kristen wasn't so sure, but she didn't let Lauren know. It was hard to argue with a woman possessed of such faith. "I agree, Lauren. Something in me knows you're both going to be healthy and whole. I really believe that." And in that moment, she did. Kristen was enveloped with a sense of peace, one telling her to stay calm and help Lauren with her caseload. That was to be her gift to Lauren, Bryan, and their baby.

"That means so much to me," Lauren whispered. "I know you don't believe in God the way I do, but I have the feeling you do at this moment."

Kristen brought her friend a muffin and herbal tea, and they settled in to review Lauren's patient load. Some were fine with delaying their therapy until after Lauren's maternity leave. Those who needed interim treatment were discussed, and Kristen felt confident she could handle their issues with competence. Lauren also offered her availability for consultation, depending on the status of the baby.

"We're down to the last patient," Lauren said. She lost eye contact with Kristen and nibbled on her muffin. "This one is tricky, but I believe you can handle her."

"What's her name?" Kristen asked. "What's tricky about her?"

"Heather Tilson." Lauren looked away again as she sipped her tea.

Kristen actually prayed for patience, which was telling since she didn't ever pray. What was Lauren thinking? Surely she could have referred Heather to another practitioner in town.

"Lauren, she caused me to lose my job! How can I treat her?" Kristen asked. "I have no objectivity. More to the point, it would open us both up to ethics complaints, which I thought was your reason for being so careful to transfer your patients as early as possible. I just don't understand."

"Hear me out," Lauren said. "I've been seeing Heather for two months. I was glad when you referred her to the GCC Counseling Center, because up to that point she hadn't been taking therapy seriously. She no-showed her appointments or cancelled at the last minute. Late charges didn't faze her – she just had her parents pay the fees. When she acted out with you, and you lost your job as a result, she had an epiphany of sorts. She wants to make things right. Since she's not your student anymore, you could see her without that conflict of interest."

Lauren's pitch was barely worthy of the worst used car salesman. Kristen wondered if this messy situation was a factor in her friend's high blood pressure. It didn't matter, though.

"Lauren Dawson, I love you and value you as one of my dearest friends," Kristen said. "But listen to yourself. What you want me to do is impossible. How can I treat Heather without the constant background memory of what she did to me? How can I be empathetic? How can we brainstorm solutions to her problems, whatever they are, without my wondering if she'll turn on me like she did only a few weeks ago?"

"You can, Kristen, I know it. You're a good person. One of the things I know about your therapeutic style is that you value the underdog and believe everyone deserves a second chance. I've thought about the ethical issues. I called Dr. Cheaney, told him the details, and he's willing to be your consultant if you take Heather on. He agreed with me that you would be up to the challenge, and he also said the ethical questions would be covered if you had a senior therapist acting as an advisor."

"I need to think about this. Lauren, you've really thrown me. If you weren't bedridden, we'd wrestle this out. Literally! My sister Katie can attest to my persuasive abilities."

"Understood. Let's schedule the three most pressing clients for tomorrow. Will that work for you? We can let Heather wait until you've had a chance to think it through. In terms of her treatment, it's actually a good idea to let her wait a bit for you to decide."

"And I can't decide until I know what's going on with her," Kristen said. "Why did she want therapy, and what changed in the last few weeks?"

"Lots of things changed at about the same time, and she couldn't handle them. The pressure of grad school applications was getting to her. She's also in a relationship with a basically good guy who can be controlling. Her controlling mother doesn't like him, which adds to his appeal to Heather. She's not sure how much she really cares for him. She just enjoys her mother's discomfort. But the biggest challenge has been Heather's pregnancy."

Kristen stared at Lauren. "Well, that's a complication, for sure. What's her plan?"

"At this point, she doesn't know. We've talked a lot about the gift of life, Heather's own goals, and how her boyfriend, Cody, will react. Heather hasn't told him yet."

Lauren stirred her tea and continued. "If you think about it,

Kristen, I'm actually not the best fit for Heather at this point. I'm pregnant, happy with my husband, but afraid that things will all end badly for my baby. I want Heather to make her own choice, which I pray is to keep the baby or put it up for adoption. But it has to be her choice, not one made from guilt because her therapist is in a high-risk pregnancy. Does that all make sense?"

It made perfect sense, Kristen thought. *But did it mean she had to be the one to treat Heather? She needed to call Dr. Cheaney.*

After the usual pleasantries, Dr. Cheaney got right to the point. "So, you're mad at me for suggesting you treat Heather, right? Let me have it."

"Not mad, but confused. No, shocked. How can it be possible for me to provide this spoiled kid with counseling services after she ruined my career at GCC? Really, Dr. Cheaney, you're being unrealistic." Kristen clenched her fists, hating to contradict her mentor's opinion.

"Good job, Kristen," he replied casually. "I'm surprised you could stand up to me. It's about time, don't you think? If you can tell me to rethink my position, which by the way, I'm not going to do, you can surely treat a bratty college senior effectively. She needs some gentle confrontation, but confrontation nonetheless."

The rest of the phone meeting went well, or so Kristen hoped. Dr. Cheaney made a good point. If she couldn't deal with Heather in an adult manner, then by extension her conflict- avoidance would tarnish her other relationships. He would be available for supervision, should she need it. She hated it when he was right!

Following a long run, Kristen pondered what to do with the rest of her day. The exercise hadn't provided her with its usual clarity of thought. She still couldn't decide what to do with Heather. Dr. Cheaney thought she was up to the task, but she had her doubts. Lauren said Heather wanted to made amends – how would that work? The dean was clear no interference would change his decision about Kristen's adjunct status. What other kind of amends could there be in this mess?

Stuck in her circular thinking, she reverted to habit. Time to build inventory. Tired of sewing, she returned to wreath construction. The sight of Sophie's unfinished wreath caught her attention. She would finish it so Sophie could have a happy memory of their work on Monday. Poor kid. Her dad went off on Kristen, and Sophie had to go home with him after Kristen's icy farewell. Upon reflection, Kristen knew she hadn't been any more mature than Mike. Her own anger got in the way. Ironic, since she was the one accusing him of having anger issues.

The wreath made her smile, despite the memory of its abrupt interruption. The tiny pink flower clusters ("That's my *Number One* color, remember?" Sophie had asked), and the glittered cornflower blue unicorns were certainly reflective of Mike's sunny, feminine little girl. The wreath needed a finishing touch, though. Wide ribbon would fuss it up too much. More greenery would make it look too heavy. Kristen thought about Sophie and her love for her father. Something pertaining to Mike needed to be on the wreath. But what?

Well, she couldn't put devil's horns or a green-faced hulk on it, so she had to be more inventive. One thing kept coming to mind. Sophie was very proud of her daddy's profession. Kristen should add something medical to the wreath, but it needed to fit into the overall whimsical feel. Kristen spotted the inspiration she sought in her crafting catalog. She rummaged through her medicine cabinet, coming up with a large empty pill bottle left over from Bernie's latest trip to the vet. She ripped off the label and printed a new one on the computer. It read: *Rx - Three hugs and two kisses, taken each morning and evening, for as long as required. Love - Daddy, MD.*

After attaching the label, Kristen carefully glued the bottle to the top center of the wreath. A few skinny ribbon curls added the perfect touch to Sophie's lovely creation. Now Kristen had to decide when to give it to her. Sophie would be at Mike's until Sunday afternoon, when he'd drive her back to Indianapolis. Lauren's phrase about Heather wanting to make things right jumped into Kristen's head. She needed to make up with Mike. He'd tried on the phone, but she'd cut him off.

And why not? He'd been a bear, assuming she would ever put Sophie in danger. But she'd been a bear in her own passive-aggressive way. Shutting the door on Mike wasn't the picture of healthy conflict management. She'd educated countless clients on voicing their feelings, even when it was tough to do. She hadn't applied that thinking to her own life yet. It was time.

Tapping his number before she lost her courage, she waited. Mike's phone went directly to voice mail. Unwilling to leave a message, or more accurately, unsure of what she would say, she ended the call.

Her phone rang as she was dishing up comfort food, some creamy boxed Alfredo noodles. *Here we go*, she thought. It was Mike.

"Kristen are you okay?" he asked, his words rushed. "I couldn't get to the phone, and you didn't leave a message. What's wrong?"

"Nothing," she said. "I finished Sophie's wreath and wanted to ask when to bring it by. I know she'll be leaving Sunday."

"Anytime is fine," Mike said. Kristen thought she heard hope in his voice, but that was probably her wishing it to be there. "As a matter of fact, Sophie and I were just leaving to pick up a pizza. We could bring it by and share if you want."

"Yes, yes, yes," Sophie said in the background, using her cute repetitive style. Kristen could visualize her jumping up and down for effect. "Let's go to Kristen's house and eat pizza with Bernie."

"That would be fine, but you don't have to share," Kristen said. "I just made some dinner."

Obviously able to hear Kristen's voice, Sophie yelled, "What did you make?"

Convinced she'd be the target of Mike's nutritional contempt, Kristen was honest. "Just some easy pasta mix. Nothing fancy."

"That's perfect with pizza! Right, Daddy?" Sophie was almost rapturous.

"Sure," Mike said. "That's great."

Kristen laughed for the first time in a few days. "Nice cover, Mike. You don't have to eat any of it, nor does Sophie. You're welcome to, but no pressure."

"We'll be there in twenty minutes," Mike said. "Or sooner, if Sophie has her way. I'm glad you called."

Kristen wasn't sure if she was glad about the call, but she was relieved. Relieved she could apologize to Mike, and relieved at his forgiving tone. Her life had sure gotten interesting since she'd met him. Annie would have a field day with this.

Chapter Eight

Mike and Sophie picked up the pizza with Sophie chattering nonstop on the way to Kristen's house. His little girl was as relieved as he was. They had both missed Kristen, though it had been only a few days since his outburst. He wondered if this visit would be brief and stilted. Kristen had only said she finished Sophie's wreath, not that she wanted to chat and eat pizza. When was he going to learn to control his outbursts? Kristen was a keeper, he suddenly realized, and he may have ruined his chance with her.

Kristen opened her door, firmly gripping the delirious Bernie. Mike carefully negotiated the front steps while carrying the large pizza box. Sophie was inside in an instant, taking Bernie off Kristen's hands.

"Let me help you with that box," Kristen said. "This is very nice of you, considering my behavior during our last conversation."

Surprised at her apologetic tone, Mike smiled. "Your behavior didn't match mine. I'm still kicking myself for seeing the glue gun and jumping to all the wrong conclusions. You've been nothing but spectacular with Sophie. I should have known better. As a matter of fact, Sophie has offered to help me think before I speak."

Kristen's light laughter was like music. "She's a bright kid, that girl of yours. She picked up on your words and used them against you. But I'm to blame, too. I've been reminded about the importance of making things right, so here we are. I've got to work on my phobic response to conflict. It's a part of life, after all. So, this is your official warning of my new approach to your anger. Understood?"

Boy, there she goes again, talking like a psychologist, Mike thought.

But there are worse things. And she wants to make up. If Sophie weren't here, we'd really be making up!

As Kristen looked at him with an arched brow, Mike realized his face had given away his desires. She turned away and pointed to the table, already set with paper plates and napkins.

"Time to eat," she said. "Sophie, I've got your milk poured. My pasta is in the serving bowl, and there's also fruit salad. Your pizza smells wonderful."

"It will be okay," Sophie said with minimal enthusiasm. "Daddy let me order half pepperoni, but then he put all kinds of veggies on the other half. Maybe you can eat that part?"

"Glad to," Kristen said. "I like veggies on pizza. You're both kind to share your dinner with me."

"Daddy was very happy you called," Sophie mumbled, her mouth full of pepperoni. "He's been sad since we were at your house making wreaths." Remembering the reason for their visit, she added, "Where is my wreath? I can't wait to see it."

"In my back bedroom," Kristen said. "Let's enjoy our food first. Okay?"

"And let's remember our manners," Mike added. "We need to thank Kristen for the side dishes she added to our meal."

When lunch and cleanup were over, Sophie declared the wreath a huge success. Mike helped her read the message on the pill container, which caused Sophie to wonder about all the missed hugs and kisses when she stayed with her mother. Mike assured her he would make them up when she was with him.

Sophie and Bernie went out to the fenced backyard to play, while Mike helped Kristen dispose of the pizza box and paper goods. He wondered what she was thinking. No matter. He knew what he was thinking. He was happy to help them both make amends.

"That wreath is terrific, Kristen," he said. "You could sell lots of those at the festival. Any little girl who loves her daddy would want one."

"Maybe. I didn't make it as a prototype. I made it for the two of you." She was using that frosty tone again.

He'd missed the mark. Time to backtrack. "That's not what I meant, and I think you know it. I'm touched by your thoughtfulness and by your awareness of how close I am to Sophie. But that's not important now. It's time for us to make up properly."

Pulling her into a corner of the kitchen, he gathered her into his arms. He kissed her forehead, temples, and neck, sensing her tremble. Finding her lips, he lingered, and then kissed her firmly. Her golden hair, falling in waves instead of curls today, brushed against his neck. Wondering what her response would be, he backed up, looking into her eyes.

Kristen looked back, which he hoped was a good sign. He'd never had this much trouble with a woman. Usually the female hospital staff members were so anxious to have him notice them he was able to take his pick, despite his obnoxious ways. Kristen was a different story.

"I'm not sure who's making amends here, but I like it," she said, interrupting his train of thought. "Michael Sutliff, you are one good kisser. But we need to talk about losing our tempers. I mean both of us. You get mad and everyone within shouting distance knows about it. I get mad and I withdraw. We both need to do better if we're going to keep this up."

"I want to keep this up," he said with a sly grin. "We need to see each other more without Sophie. My parents are back in town, and she's staying with them tonight. Do you have plans? Could we have a real date? No Sophie in the back seat, no meeting my x-wife, no walking on eggshells. Just the two of us."

"That sounds lovely," Kristen said.

Before she could launch into any more psych talk, he kissed her again. This time he took longer, massaging the tension in her shoulders as he found her lips. She brought her arms around his neck, lightly dancing her fingers along his shirt collar.

She must have forgiven him. She was kissing him back. They had a date. Life was looking up.

Mike dropped Sophie off at his parents' house after lunch. She brought her wreath to show them, describing every detail with pride. Of course, she also told them about his reaction to the glue gun.

"Daddy thought I was using a real hot glue gun, and he yelled at Kristen," she tattled.

"I'm sure he was just worried about your safety," Jane said. "But Kristen wouldn't put you in any danger."

"Duh, Grandma," Sophie declared. "Daddy should have known that."

Feeling chastened, Mike kissed Sophie goodbye. "I'll pick you up tomorrow after church. We can meet in our usual spot in the parking lot," he said. "Mom, thanks for watching her overnight. Call me if anything comes up."

"What could come up?" his mother asked. "She's going to have a grand time, as usual. Anita will fret, but she'll get over it."

Knowing Sophie would be well fed and overdosed on sugar, Mike shook his head. After cleaning up and doing some weekend chores, he headed to Kristen's, wondering if he was doing a good job raising Sophie. Partially raising her was more accurate. The divorce continued to nag at him. He knew Anita was happy now with Grant. He was happy, too, now that Kristen was in his life. But feelings of failure washed over him, as they had millions of times since his marriage ended. He had failed at one of the most important relationships in life. What did that make him?

God forgave all sins, he knew. He had to hold on to that for now. His single-minded focus on medical school and training was the primary factor in the divorce. In fact, his med school orientation staff had warned the class about the risk to marriages. Of course, as newly admitted med students, all at the top of their college classes, they were convinced it would never happen to them. They were invincible, or so they thought.

Kristen seemed to sense his mood as he held the car door for her. She looked great in her black halter dress. She thought this date was important, and he was grateful for that.

"What's up, Mike?" she asked, settling into the leather seat. "You're in a funk of some sort."

"Sorry. You're right. I had one of my waves of guilt about my divorce. I'm a real suave date, huh?"

Kristen stared as he pulled onto Gordon's main street. "Would you like my opinion, or will you resent my psych talk?"

She sure had his number. He'd risk it though. "Your opinion. I think."

"I believe your guilt, or whatever you call it, is actually grief. You've gone through the feelings of anger, failure, and shame. Now you're at the sad part. Your dream of a long life with Anita and Sophie is over. It's a huge loss. You have to acknowledge that loss before you can realize a new dream can come along. A dream that's just as good, only different."

Mike's hands gripped the wheel. It was fortunate they were in small town Gordon, not Indianapolis. It was hard to focus on the road. He'd asked for her opinion, and he got it. It galled him that she was probably right.

"Well put, Kristen," he said. "I don't know what it is – guilt, grief, or whatever. But I don't like it at all. How about if we shelve this topic for now? Let's enjoy our dinner, and the surprise I have planned."

"Fine. Avoidance can be a strategy, as long as you don't get stuck in it," Kristen said. "Where are we going? I'm starved."

His choice of a country-style restaurant off a side highway seemed to please her. The menu was varied enough that she could have pot roast while he enjoyed his salmon. Each entrée was cooked to perfection. He noticed Kristen seemed to relax. They talked about everything but Sophie. Kristen expanded on her unsettled life.

"My work situation continues to be complex," Kristen said. "I've built a good inventory of crafts, so the festival in October isn't as scary to me as it was a month ago. Lauren Gardner has taken maternity leave early, and as a result I've already begun seeing a few of her clients. She may be admitted to the hospital tomorrow due to her blood pressure. Say a prayer, would you? She and Bryan have waited a long time for that baby."

"I'll pray for Lauren," Mike said. "There's also a chance I'll meet her when I go back on service Monday. I'll ask God for guidance for my care, too."

Kristen blinked, a single tear falling down her cheek. He took her hand across the table, holding it as she looked at him. "Thanks, Mike. I'm sorry to cry. Things pile up. I know I need a break when I'm tearful like this."

"Don't be sorry to cry," he said. "You just told me I needed to acknowledge my losses. You do, too. You've lost a job you love, a friend is in crisis, and you're charting a new professional path. Your dad is gone, and your mom's across the country. Hard stuff, all of it."

"Now who's talking like a psychologist?" Kristen teased. Her equilibrium returned, and they looked at the dessert menu. After deciding to share the carrot cake, she stared at him.

"Did you say something about a surprise? What's up? I'm not sure I can take anything too eventful."

"You'll see after dinner," Mike said. He smiled and hoped he could help Kristen deal with her struggles. He realized he cared about her in a way he hadn't thought possible after his divorce. She was more fragile than she let on. He wanted the best for her. He also loved kissing her.

The restaurant had a walking path bordered with flowers behind the side entrance. Mike and Kristen enjoyed the chance to walk off dinner while viewing the wonder of summer in Indiana. It had been hot, and the flowers looked a little seedy but bright. Mike used the vista to talk about his faith.

"You're right about my sense of grief," he said. "Another thing I'm having trouble with is breaking my wedding vows. Anita and I were married in church with all the trappings. 'For better or worse' seems to have been forgotten by both of us."

"Not by you, I can tell," Kristen said. "You're still full of faith, but you can't reconcile how the marriage turned out. Have you talked to your minister about all this?"

"I've thought about it. Maybe I should. On my next week off I'll schedule with Reverend Taylor."

"One more thing," Kristen said. "Anita was part of the divorce, too. I'm not placing blame. In my experience, there's usually plenty to go around. Of course, when I say that, the couple usually asks if I'm married. My credibility goes down when I say I'm single!"

"As a physician, I haven't had every disease known to man, but I can treat many of them. Isn't that the same for you?"

"It should be, but when people are angry or feeling misunderstood, it's an easy place to land. That is, what would I know about marital problems if I've never been there?"

"That's why I like medicine," Mike said. "I can order blood values or imaging tests and have a sense of what's going on with a patient. You, on the other hand, have to ask questions, intuit, and theorize."

"Admit it, you do the same," Kristen said. "I think the point is we both have challenging jobs. On to other things. Where's my surprise?"

Patting his pocket, Mike set the stage. "You don't have to use this. I wanted you to have it though, because as I've gotten to know you, I thought it fit. You have so many talents and gifts."

"Now I'm really intrigued. What is it?" Kristen looked like a kid at Christmas. He could get used to this. Her anticipation had a sexy quality he wanted to see more of.

Mike pulled out the tissue-wrapped box. Kristen unwrapped it and looked inside. It held engraved desk nameplate that read:

Kristen Anderson, Ph.D.
Psychologist and Artisan

This time two tears made their way down Kristen's cheeks. She looked at Mike with a befuddled smile. "I love it, Mike. Thank you. It means so much. More than you can know."

"Good," he said, reaching for her free hand. "You don't have to display it in your office. Patients may ask what it means. It could interfere with the flow of your sessions."

"That's okay. If it becomes a distraction, I'll display it at home. I will never put it in a drawer or closet, though. It means too much to me."

Mike squeezed Kristen's hand and kissed her. He was thrilled his risk had been successful. Anita had always harped that he didn't appreciate her professional work, so he was determined not to make the same mistake with Kristen. He also wondered if he would always make decisions with Kristen based on past experiences with Anita. It was like walking a tightrope. He dared to hope he and Kristen could forge their own relationship, free of their pasts.

As they continued their peaceful walk, Kristen's phone jingled. She checked the ID, and said, "It's my mom. I need to take this in case something's wrong."

"Of course," Mike said.

From the part of the conversation he was able to hear, he guessed Mrs. Anderson was the chatty type. He also noticed Kristen's careful questions about her mother's social life. He zoned out until her heard Kristen tell her mother not to interfere with the dean. Now he was curious.

Kristen finished with her mother, frowning. "I'm sorry, Mike. My mother means well, but she rattles me sometimes. Long story short, you know about the student dispute that caused the dean to put me on adjunct status. I didn't tell you my mother turned the dean down when he asked for a date not long after my dad died. Mom wants me to add that to the HR report, if I choose to make one."

"Your mother has a point," Mike said. "You're being punished unfairly at several levels. The student acted out and got away with it. Now it seems the dean is acting out as well."

"True. I'm still not ready to go to HR, though. To your credit, you're one of several people to say I should. I'll keep thinking about it. But first I have to manage my life for the next few months. I'm balancing a lot."

"That you are," Mike said, pulling her close. "I'm hoping I'm one of the things on your list. You're certainly on my list of important people."

Kristen smiled, gazing into his eyes. "Yes, Mike, you're definitely on my list of things to balance."

Wolfing down his quick pre-church breakfast of toast with jelly, Mike marveled at Kristen's tenacity. Most people with her crazy life would be at the end of their rope. Her strength was impressive, but he wondered about her hesitation to file a work complaint with the GCC Human Resources department. She seemed to be worried about making the situation worse. Maybe the small college didn't have the sharpest folks in HR.

As he pulled on his sport coat, he also speculated about the social sciences dean. That fellow certainly didn't sound too sharp either. Punishing Kristen after being rebuffed by her mother was so middle school. And what kind of creep would make advances on a new widow? Maybe he also had a thing for Kristen. Mike could sure see the attraction, and he was determined to help her. He'd figure something out.

After church, Mike and his parents handled the "Sophie transfer" with ease. She had so many things at the elder Sutliff home that forgetting an item or two wasn't a problem. Sophie planted wet kisses on her grandparents, with additional air kisses for them as Mike pulled away in his car. They settled in for the lengthy drive.

"Daddy, tell me everything you did while I was gone," Sophie said. "I bet you and Kristen had fun together."

"Who said we were together?" he asked.

"I did. I know you like her, and she likes you. You probably needed to have dinner without me. Right?"

"Right. Sophie, have you ever thought about being a lawyer when you grow up? You ask a lot of pointed questions."

"Never mind about me growing up. Did you take Kristen to a nice place? Mommy says you guys only ate at burger places because you didn't have any money. You can take Kristen somewhere better, huh?"

Mike's jaw twitched. Anita hadn't bothered to educate Sophie about the exorbitant cost of medical school. Nor had she explained she was the one who liked fast food burgers. Mike would have been happy with a turkey sandwich at home. He would be the grown-up, though. Especially since he was the only one in the car.

"Mommy thought burgers were a treat," he told his daughter. "But she's right about not having much money. All my schooling cost a lot. Kristen and I had a nice dinner, but nothing too fancy."

Sophie seemed satisfied with his response. She launched into an extensive review of her night with Grandma and Grandpa. In addition to the expected diet of sweets and treats, she watched two of her favorite movies.

"And I'm not supposed to tell you this, Daddy," she said. "I got to stay up until ten o'clock. *P.M.* I'm not even fussy today, am I?"

"Not yet," he said. "I'd be wanting a snooze if I were you. But I'm happy we can talk as I drive."

He loved it when his tricks worked, which happened more and more rarely. Five minutes later Sophie was sleeping in her booster car seat, which gave him time to gear up for his visit with Anita and Grant.

As expected, Anita was waiting at the door when he and Sophie pulled up. Maybe Anita missed Sophie as much as he did when she was gone. Or maybe Anita wanted to see if Kristen was with them. He was still trying to decide if the two women had gotten along, but it had been a short meeting. Time would tell.

"How was your drive, sweetie?" Anita asked Sophie.

"It was good, Mommy. I slept a lot of the way. Daddy says I snore, but I think he's teasing."

Anita smiled at Mike. "Yes, he's teasing you, honey. If anyone in that car can snore, it's not you, believe me."

Mike laughed. "I've been caught, Sophie. I have been known to snore, but I've never heard you do it. You're a very lady-like sleeper."

Sophie's suitcase was unpacked, and Anita offered drinks and snacks. Both parents were happy to see Sophie reach for cheese chunks and fruit slices on the tray Anita had prepared. A month ago Sophie would have refused a snack.

Anita motioned Mike to follow her to the kitchen and said, "Sophie's been doing a lot better, don't you think? She's eating and sleeping more consistently. I've actually had to buy her a few pieces of clothing a size up from last month. And Grant isn't complaining about her either – they're enjoying each other most of the time."

"I agree," he said. "It's a credit to both of us, and to Sophie's ability to adapt. I'll admit I've been having a lot of guilt lately about her being split between us."

Anita studied his face, patting him gently on the cheek. "Mike, we did our best. We tried, sort of, in counseling. But apart from the hours away from each other due to your studies, I think we're fundamentally not suited for the long haul. Grant and I spend quiet evenings. We read, binge on Netflix, and eat a simple dinner. When she's with us, Sophie is fine with that. You're much too active for such a life. I think that's why you've adjusted so well to the hospitalist schedule. It's go-go-go for twelve hours. That's perfect for you. I'd be in a puddle on the floor!"

"Are you saying Sophie shouldn't stay with me as much?" Mike asked.

"No, not at all. I was worried at first that she'd come back from Gordon an overtired mess, but she's thrived. I think after your week at work, you're able to relax with her. Kristen is a part of that, too. Right?"

Unsure about how much to reveal, Mike hedged. "Kristen's

great with Sophie, but she's not her nanny or anything. They're not together that much."

"Relax, Mike. As always, you jump to the defensive position. I like Kristen. Sophie likes her. From what I've heard, they interact well. I'm glad you've found a woman to share your life with."

"What? You've got us seriously committed, and I've only known Kristen since the Fourth of July. Give it a rest, Anita."

"Yep. Just as I thought," Anita said with a smug grin. "You're in deeper than you think."

"Okay, I like her a lot. But this time around, I've got to be sure. I can't put Sophie through another divorce. I thank God daily you've found a good man in Grant, and that he loves Sophie. You'll laugh, but I've been seeking wisdom in the Bible. The Proverbs 31 woman is my guide for my future spouse."

Anita did laugh. For almost two full minutes. After she wiped her tears and the fluid running out of her nose, she was able to respond. "Mike, honey, good luck with that Proverbs thing. Any woman worth her salt will call you out on that pronto. Any Proverbs *men* out there? Shouldn't you be looking inward? What does the Bible say about a godly man?"

Mike hated it when Anita made a good point. Perhaps, just perhaps, he was focusing too much on Kristen's attributes and not enough on his own. He knew God was using this moment to humble him. He went with it.

"What godly qualities should I work on, Anita?" he asked. "You know me better than anyone except my mother. My mom's probably not objective."

Anita's look was fierce. "You bet she's not," she said. "Because I will always love you as Sophie's father, I'll answer your question. According to my limited knowledge of the Bible, a godly man should love the Lord, be just and trustworthy, have moderate habits, and not be prone to wrath."

Mike thought for a minute. "I think I fit pretty well, except for the moderation and wrath parts. I work too much, or I did in the past, and my temper can still be an issue."

"I agree," Anita said. "That's part of why I like Kristen. She seems to even you out a little. I'll bet her reaction to your temper has gotten your attention."

Wondering how Anita knew that, Mike was about to ask her when Sophie bounded in to the kitchen, with Grant following. "I heard Kristen's name. Is she coming to Indianapolis? I miss her. Kristen and Daddy had grown-up time last night."

Anita, then Grant, arched their brows. Grant also grunted.

"Our grown-up time was only dinner, as I told you, Sophie. We ate at that country kitchen place, Anita. Home cooking at its finest. You never did like it, as I recall," Mike said.

"Very funny," Anita shot back. "I just remembered another quality of a godly man. He should not be belligerent or snarky." Now Mike laughed.

"I'm not sure 'snarky' is in the Bible," he said as he headed to his car for the drive back to Gordon. "Anyway, have a great week, you three. I'll see you soon."

Mike loved to drive alone. The first few hours after dropping off Sophie were always lonely, but he had a chance to think as he put the car on cruise control for the long stretch of highway leading to Gordon.

He admitted to himself he had some changing to do in terms of being a godly man. Kristen had suggested talking to Reverend Taylor about his grief over the divorce. Maybe he could also ask about changing bad habits and improving his character. He remembered all the courses in med school addressing behavior change. Usually people didn't make big changes until they hit bottom. Was his relationship with Kristen important enough to cause him to change? If he drove her away, would that be his rock bottom?

It would, he realized. *Without her, I'd be more than lonely. I'd be lost.*

Chapter Nine

Monday dawned rainy and humid. Kristen hadn't slept much, tossing around in bed as she concocted different scenarios for Heather's therapy visit later today. Lauren had suggested having Heather wait until later in the week for her session, but the young woman had called, almost begging for a Monday appointment with Kristen.

Kristen dressed carefully, choosing tailored slacks topped by a professional blazer. Her "power look" was for her benefit, not Heather's. Kristen needed as much authority and confidence as she could muster. She also wanted to show Heather she was still standing despite Heather's visit to the dean.

In contrast to her behavior with Lauren, Heather was early for her session. Kristen entered the building lobby, greeted the office assistant, and then told Heather she would be ready for her in a few minutes. Kristen booted up her computer, surveyed her counseling office, and marched back to the waiting area to escort Heather in.

Heather looked better than she had when they'd last met in Kristen's office at GCC. She was dressed in casual slacks, a long floral top, and flip-flops. Typical college senior attire, but Heather also looked rested and well-groomed. Kristen hoped these changes were all good signs.

When they were seated, Heather began. "Dr. Anderson, thanks for seeing me. I'll say up front this will be our only session. Is that okay?"

"Whatever you need," Kristen replied. *What was going on here?*

"I wanted to meet with you away from campus. I need to apologize for my behavior in your office, and with the dean. I'd just learned I was pregnant, and then I got my exam back with your comments. I was an idiot. I'll admit it. You made good points about my essay response, but I couldn't hear them. I was in shock. I probably should have gone back to the doctor, because I was thinking about doing some drastic things. But I'm better now."

"Keep going," Kristen said. "I'm listening, though I will say I'm glad you're feeling better."

"After our meeting, and after I ratted you out to the dean, I told my boyfriend I was pregnant. Cody was great. He was so happy, and he reminded me he loved me and wanted to get married. When he'd first proposed, I'd put him off. I was going to be the great grad student and had no time for a husband. But now everything is different. This baby has reminded me there's more to life than school and grades."

Heather's face confirmed her words. She was glowing in the way novels always described pregnant women. Kristen smiled.

"I'm happy for you, Heather. Your life is changing fast, but you seem to be at peace. May I ask you some questions?"

"Sure. But before you do, I want you to know I went back to the dean and tried to explain I was out of line about your grade on my exam. He wouldn't see me. His administrative assistant put me off by saying he was too busy. But I could hear him through the open door, chatting on the phone with a buddy while they set up a golf date. And I know he heard me, too."

"Thanks for trying. There may be more going on than you think in this situation. But it helps me to know you made the effort to explain your reaction to the test grade."

Kristen continued. "Now for my questions. First, and most important, you mentioned some drastic thoughts when you found out you were pregnant. What were they?"

"I thought about all the predictable things," Heather said, looking down at her hands. "My pregnancy was early enough to get an abortion, but I couldn't do that. I thought about doing myself in, so I wouldn't bring shame to my family. Do you know my mother prides herself on coming from a family with no divorce and no 'premature' babies?"

"Oh dear," Kristen said. "That's a lot of pressure for you."

"Mom is something. But when I told Cody, it all came into focus. I want this baby, and I want a life with Cody. He's a good man – sexy, loving, and tolerant of my craziness. I love him very much. What I thought I didn't like about him was just his reaction to my mom's meddling in our relationship. Mom didn't like that Cody's dad works as a mechanic, so she thought he wasn't good enough for me."

Once again, Heather's presentation matched her statements about Cody. Dreamy, excited, floating on air – all the romantic descriptors fit Heather's face and body language.

"How is your relationship now with your mother?" Kristen asked. "Have you told her and your dad about the pregnancy? And your plan to marry?"

"Cody and I visited them last night. Mom was her usual hysterical self, but my dad stepped up. Cody had already called Dad and asked for permission to marry me. That went a long way with my traditional father. So eventually Mom settled down. She's already called Gordon's best wedding planner. We've set a date for four weeks from this weekend, during fall break at GCC. I'll finish the semester and graduate in December. I've got loads of extra course credit, so it all works out."

"Congratulations, Heather. You've shown a lot of courage in a difficult situation. I'm sure you'll be happy with Cody. And you've answered all my questions except for one. Where do you stand with your plans for grad school?"

"I'll wait until the baby is old enough for daycare," Heather said. "Cody will graduate in May, so lots will depend on where he gets a job. But I'll get to grad school eventually, I know it."

"Yes, you will. One of my grad school professors didn't get her doctorate until she was almost forty. She built a great career and often said her life experience helped her be a better psychologist. As a matter of fact, there are graduate programs that won't admit students straight out of their undergraduate degree programs. You'll be a fine psychologist when the time is right."

Heather smiled but stayed put. She hesitated, looking tentatively at Kristen. "Thanks, Dr. Anderson. I started by saying this would be our only session. But can I change that? With Lauren on maternity leave and with my life so crazy right now, could I stay on your client list? In case I need to check in or have issues with my mom?"

"Sure you can," Kristen said. "You know how to reach me. I just need your promise that if you get any more 'drastic thoughts,' you'll call first and not act on them."

"It's a promise," Heather said. "Can I ask you a question now?"

Kristen nodded, wondering what was coming.

"Since I caused you to lose your job, are you going to be okay?"

"I'm fine," Kristen said. "And as I said earlier, there were other factors in play with the dean. I can't talk about them, but rest assured your complaint wasn't the entire reason he acted the way he did."

"When Dean Benson blew me off, my mom suggested I meet with the provost to explain why I was so unreasonable about my exam grade. Would you be upset if I did that?"

"Not at all. Even if it goes nowhere, I'm grateful for your efforts. But be sure to focus on your own health for now, Heather. And you've got a wedding to plan!"

Heather left Kristen's office, clearly relieved the session had gone well. Kristen shared that sentiment – she hadn't known what to expect from the volatile young woman. She was surprised at Heather's apology, but also knew Heather's future wasn't going to be as rosy as the bride-to-be assumed. There were huge adjustments to be made – to marriage, to parenthood, and who knew what else?

Life will challenge her in new ways, Kristen thought. *As it does with all of us.*

Client appointments consumed most of the day. Kristen filled the gaps between appointments with paperwork and insurance calls. This part of psychotherapy was the necessary evil involved when helping others. Kristen found doing the bulk of paperwork on Mondays was most efficient for her. She was fresh and motivated to argue the need for services with reluctant insurance carriers.

Later, as she unlocked her door, fending off Bernie's jumps and kisses, her phone rang. Katie's picture flashed. Kristen let Bernie relieve himself in the back yard and took her sister's call. After the usual pleasant banter, Katie got to the point.

"I thought Mom was better," she said. "But she's so unpredictable. Last week she was logical and open about how much she missed Dad. Yesterday morning, though, she was tearful about some slight from another resident, and she was ready to marry her new friend so they could have a place of their own. Then this afternoon, she called and could barely string a sentence together. Kristen, she wasn't making any sense. She almost sounded drunk, but we know she doesn't drink. I just got back from visiting her, and now I'm even more confused. When I got there, Mom was fine – she'd had a sandwich and was drinking some iced tea while she watched her favorite game show. She couldn't imagine why I had driven all the way from my house to see her, since we'd just talked." Katie drew a long breath. "I've about had it," she whispered.

Kristen was alarmed, too. "Wow, this is scary. Mom's never been like this. She's been erratic at times, but not this uneven. Do you know how recently she's seen a doctor?"

"She had a physical prior to moving to the apartment," Katie said. "She checked out well. I was with her and heard the doctor's feedback. His only recommendation was for Mom to lose a little weight."

"She's been dieting?" Kristen asked. "I wonder if that's a factor in her behavior."

"Who knows?" Katie said. "I guess I'll try to get her an appointment with the doctor. Any chance you could come out and help me?"

Kristen paused. She'd been telling herself having no full-time job offered her tons of flexibility. Maybe she should use some of her free time to help her mother and sister.

"Katie, call the doctor and get an appointment for early next week. I can fly out this Saturday, come to the appointment with you and Mom, and fly back in time to see clients at the end of next week."

"You're an angel. Mom responds to you better than she does me. If she knows you're coming because you're worried, she won't fight me about going to the doctor. I'll text you when I have the appointment."

That settled, Kristen booked a flight from Indianapolis to Phoenix. At least the flight was direct, requiring no connections, and therefore no risk of lost luggage. Although it was only Monday evening, her week was filling up. She'd have to focus on crafting during the next few days. Her adjunct courses would meet for the first session soon, requiring all the usual prep work.

It will all work out, she told herself. *It always does. God will help. I can't believe I'm trusting God in this. Mike's faith is rubbing off on me. Lauren's too.*

Her phone dingled again, this time identifying Mike as the caller.

"How was your Monday?" he asked. "Mine was busy, but good. Your friend Lauren says hello. I can't tell you more than that, though. You might want to pay her a visit."

"I will. I hope she and the baby are okay. You can't tell me anything?"

"Unfortunately, I can't. Give her a call when we're finished. She'd love to hear from you. In other news, how is your weekend shaping up? Any time for me?"

"Only Friday night," Kristen said. She filled Mike in on her mother's latest crisis. "My flight's at seven on Saturday morning. I'll get back the middle of next week."

"I'd love for you to fit me in Friday then. What would be fun for you? Or do you want to stay in since you'll be flying early the next day?"

"Any change in my routine is fun," Kristen said. *Anything with you is fun*, she thought.

"Okay, how about another road trip? You'll be in Indianapolis the next morning, so we should head in a different direction. Have you ever eaten at the new restaurant on Lake Monroe? It's ocean to table, which is quite a feat in Indiana. Their website says they don't have any freezers."

"That would be great," Kristen said while she poured Bernie's dinner into his bowl.

"You don't sound too great. If you're worried about Lauren, I'll hedge and say the news about her baby is promising. What else is going on?"

"My day went well, but it was stressful. I can't talk about my work either, as you know. But I'm fine."

Bernie barked his "You'd better take me out pronto since I've wolfed down my chow" bark. "Mike, I've got to go. Dog duty calls. I'll see you on Friday."

"See you then," Mike said as he ended the call. His tone was flat, and Kristen knew he felt shut out.

What am I supposed to do? she wondered. *I can't talk about my convoluted day, except for filling him in about Mom. He'd better get used to that if we're going to be together.*

Bernie's post-dinner walk around the neighborhood was interrupted by several stops with neighborhood kids wanting to pet him. Finally home, Kristen focused on her goal of creating three items per day for the festival. Obviously, today she was three short of the mark. What was easy to make and easy to sell?

Ornaments were the obvious answer. She'd bought several yards of red and green felt when she'd replenished her craft materials. Perfect. Kristen whipped out her shears, quickly cutting red poinsettia leaves, with about half the number of green leaves. Assembly-line style, she knotted them together to form the Christmas flower and then hot-glued silver bead clusters to each center.

Voila! She now had a dozen ornaments to sell at two dollars

each. Calculating her cost of materials, she would clear around twenty dollars. Not great, but a fair evening's work considering the day she'd had. How could she increase her profit? A quick online search revealed the solution. Gluing red and green plaid ribbon loops to the back of each ornament turned them into napkin holders. They were easy sales at five dollars each. If she had time in the coming weeks, she'd stitch up more napkins to put in them and raise the price.

Congratulating herself on being a savvy businesswoman, she was alerted by Bernie's bark at the front door. This was his "I'm defending my turf" bark, considerably more threatening than after dinner.

The doorbell chimed, and as Kristen grabbed Bernie's harness, Mike walked in.

"Don't you lock the door after dark?" he asked. "Bernie is a good watchdog, but you need to be more careful."

"Don't you usually call before dropping in? We just talked, after all. What's going on?"

Mike reddened. "I was worried about you. You had a tough day, but I couldn't help. So I came by."

"That's sweet, I think," Kristen grumbled. "What made you think I couldn't handle my tough day on my own? I've had a fair number of them lately."

"That's my point. You're handling so much with no back-up. What can I do?"

"You can give Bernie a stomach rub while I clean up this crafting mess. It's a good thing I just finished my daily quota, or you'd really be in trouble." Though her words were meant to be light-hearted, Kristen was still annoyed.

Mike got the picture. "Bernie will be occupied for as long as you need him to be. After that, would you like to grab a coffee? Or a frozen yogurt?"

"Coffee after noon keeps me up for hours. Frozen yogurt might be nice. I forgot to eat dinner."

"Boy, you have had a difficult day. I'm amazed that the nutrition guru, Dr. Kristen Anderson, has forgotten to eat a meal."

"Sarcasm will get you nowhere," Kristen said as she brandished her scissors. She had to admit Mike was right. The day had worn her down. She never forgot to eat. Never!

"Before we go, I need to call Lauren," she said. "I was going to do that after I finished up."

Kristen was relieved to hear her friend's upbeat tone. "Baby boy is doing well," she said. "My blood pressure has gone down. They want me to stay in the hospital for at least another week. Then they may induce me. But God will provide protection, as He already has."

"That faith of yours is powerful. I've got to get me some!"

"It's in you, girl," Lauren said softly. "You're a woman of faith, but you don't know its source yet. On another note, how was Heather today?"

"Can't really talk," Kristen hedged. "Let's just say it went better than I'd imagined. I'll fill you in when I visit. I had her sign a release of information form with your name on it to keep things by-the-book, even though she's going to be your patient again after your maternity leave."

"You must have company. Anyone I know? Maybe a doctor with movie-star looks? He checked on me today and raved about you."

"Yes, I have to go, too," Kristen said. Lauren's laugh filled the phone as Kristen tapped the red button.

As they ate their frozen yogurt on the stools outside the Freezy Breezy, Mike looked concerned. Kristen piped up. "My counselor empathy signals say you're worried, Mike. I'm doing well, really. I can't convince you of it, but it's true."

"I agree. It's something else. It occurred to me while you talked with Lauren about the patient that you could be in danger from your profession. What if someone has a violent partner? What if some creep stalks you after evening sessions? How do you protect yourself?"

"Those things can happen to anyone these days. I'm careful with my referrals. I purposely don't accept those who need a full mental health support system instead of a solo therapist. And I have a buddy from high school on the police force should things get troublesome."

"Very clinically stated," Mike said as he dug into his yogurt. "What you're not saying is that you have a potentially dangerous job. Have you ever thought about making crafts your full-time business?"

"You mean waste years of training? Let go of my passion? What's gotten into you, Mike? Should you quit medicine because of all the emergency room shootings? You're making no sense."

Mike took a deep breath. "No, I wouldn't leave my profession. But you mean a lot to me, Kristen. If we were to have a marriage or a family someday, I'd want to be sure you were safe. I'd want you to focus on me, Sophie, and any other children who might enter the picture. I think I have a right to hope for that. And yes, I think that does make sense."

Astonished, Kristen stared hard at Mike. What was wrong with this guy? His killer looks belied his caveman approach to relationships. Did he want her barefoot and pregnant, gluing felt for the rest of her life? Was she to be a nanny-mommy to Sophie with no other interests beyond the home?

Shaking her head, Kristen tried to be fair. After all, he had admitted he cared for her, and even mentioned marriage which was a big deal for him. "Mike, I disagree with most of what you just said. But I'm tired, stressed, and was planning to binge-watch old Christmas movies when you came over. Maybe we should continue this discussion another time. A time when we're both thinking more clearly."

"I'm thinking crystal clear," Mike said. "But I know I've upset you. Just to be certain, are you upset about meaning a lot to me or the other stuff?"

"The other stuff. You mean a lot to me, too, Mike. But we've got a lot of ground to cover before we get more serious. I'm not sure where you're getting your rigid notions about the ideal family.

Marriages and families are two-way streets where I come from. But as you said, I'm upset and it's time for me to get home and into bed. I'm really beat."

And I'm really confused, she thought as Mike drove her home. *I thought he was different from Rob. But I stood up for myself, which is progress, right?*

Kristen's Saturday flight to Arizona was smooth. She managed to watch a newly released movie, which in her mind counted as an efficient use of her time. Katie picked her up, full of joy at seeing her big sister.

"Mom's been the ideal senior lately," Katie said. "She's beyond thrilled you're coming to visit her. She even wants to introduce you to her doctor, since he's single and told her he's ready to settle down."

"She should introduce him to you. Unless you've been holding out on me. Do you have a guy in your life?"

"As a matter of fact, I do. He's a respiratory therapist at the hospital. We met at a church singles group. He's seems to be the real deal." Katie stared at the desert highway clipping by. "What about you? Anybody Mom should know about?"

"No! There's a guy, a doctor at the hospital. But we're in the 'figuring out if you're worth more time' phase. Mom would never understand. She'd have my bridal shower planned by tomorrow."

"Yes, my savvy sister, you have our mother figured out perfectly," Katie said as she dodged the dusty waste in the road. "I'll keep quiet."

The three Anderson women had a wonderful weekend. Shopping, eating Tex-Mex, and being lazy by Katie's apartment pool filled the hours. The bond they still shared, despite the absence of her father, heartened Kristen. She observed her mother carefully, unable to find any memory gaps or illogical thinking. Maybe her odd behavior could be explained simply. Grief could be overwhelming. Time should help. Mike had told her that – too bad he wasn't as wise about relationships as he was about grief and loss.

On Monday afternoon they headed to Dr. Wheeler's office. In the waiting room, which was thankfully empty, Kaye did an expert sales job on Kristen, extoling the doctor's professional and personal attributes. Kristen wouldn't be swayed.

"Mom, he sounds wonderful. But our goal here is to make sure you're okay. I live across the country, remember?"

"An insignificant matter," Kaye replied. "People move all the time. Look at me and Katie."

Before Kaye could book a moving van for Kristen, they were called into the exam room. Dr. Wheeler examined Kaye carefully, asking specific questions about her diet.

"You told me to lose some weight," Kaye said. "I've been following the whole low-carb, raw food diet thing. It worked well at first, but lately in the evening I get ravenous. I end up eating as many calories from dinner to bedtime as the rest of the day."

"That helps me understand what's going on, Mrs. Anderson," Dr. Wheeler said. "Your blood sugar tests have told the same story. Your glucose levels vary widely. My sense is you get hypoglycemic in the evenings, then eat too much, further aggravating your sugar levels. You probably feel better after a balanced dinner, right? One that includes a few foods with carbohydrates? And your outlook may be better when you're eating from all the food groups."

"You mean I'm diabetic? Both my parents were. My father had to have the shots, but my mother just took a pill. When my father's sugar was low, he was a bear. We stayed away from him until he had his juice."

"It's too early to diagnose diabetes, but my guess is you're pre-diabetic. Based on your blood tests, I'd like to start you on the lowest dose of an oral medication. I'll see you again in a month. We'll do more blood work then. However, and this is very important, you have to meet with the dietitian and follow the diet she gives you. No more avoiding carbs. Is that something you'll agree to?"

"Yes, Dr. Wheeler, I agree. I realize I've scared my girls with some of the things I've said on the phone. Maybe my diet was to blame. But it got me a visit from Kristen!"

Each daughter rolled her eyes in tandem as Dr. Wheeler laughed.

He's a cutie, Kristen thought. *But Mike is better looking. Mike also seems smarter, more seasoned as a physician. Good grief, I sound like a sixth-grader with a crush! And I'm supposed to be annoyed with Mike, the pre-historic guy who wants me to quit my job.*

Back in Gordon later that week and relieved that her mother seemed better, Kristen prepped for a busy few days. She had Lauren's patients to see, courses to prepare for, and the lingering discomfort about Mike. She did care for him, as she'd told him, but she couldn't reconcile his idea of a perfect wife. What would she be without her patients and students? She knew her identity was more than her work, but her work was a big part of who she was. She made a difference in her patients' lives. Why couldn't Mike understand that?

Chapter Ten

Mike was finishing his supper in the hospital cafeteria when the chief medical officer sat at his table. Tom Wilson was a veteran physician rumored to be thinking about retirement. He and Mike had met a few times but had no relationship beyond that of casual colleagues.

What's going on? Mike thought. *Did my tangle with Annie's nursing students get me in trouble?*

Tom began. "Mike, we've been very impressed with your work here at Gordon Memorial. Sometimes docs from the big city have a hard time adjusting to our small-town culture. My sources speak well of you and your clinical skills."

Mike had to be honest. "Tom, I appreciate that. I'll admit I had a rough start here. Some of it was personal adjustment to Gordon, some was professional. But now I enjoy my patients and the staff I work with."

"That said," Tom continued, "would you be interested in changing your role a bit? I plan to retire at the end of the year. Chief of the medical staff is a demanding role, but one I know you could fill easily. Despite the sometimes overwhelming tasks, it comes with some perks. You could work five days per week, in eight-hour shifts. No more twelve-hour days with two meals eating cafeteria food. And except for the occasional crisis call, no more weekends."

"It's all very tempting. I'd get to see my daughter more regularly, but not with the long days I have with her now. On the other hand, she'll be starting school in a few weeks, and our time together was going to be limited by that."

"I like that your first thought was about family. Trust me, you'll be better able to focus on loved ones if you're not totally exhausted after seven days of working dawn to dusk."

"That sounds good. But what about the job itself? Would I still get to see patients? How much of an administrative role would I have? Managing doctors must be like herding cats."

Tom laughed, his generous belly causing the Formica-topped table to wobble. "Maybe you don't need what I was going to offer next after all," he said. "You're right – my biggest challenges have been the ones involving personnel. But the Gordon Memorial lawyer is very savvy about physicians and their quirks. He's helped me through some tough issues."

"What were you going to offer? You know, that I might not need?"

"There's a training in a few weeks, in Grand Cayman of all places. You and your family could all go. The program is designed for future CMOs. I found it very valuable when I was starting out. And the best part is the schedule. You're in meetings with your cohort from breakfast until early afternoon. That leaves the rest of the afternoon and evening to be with your family. It's virtually a full week of vacation at the hospital's expense."

"You probably know I'm divorced. I'll need child care if I take Sophie."

"Or you could bring a child care provider," Tom replied. "That person's expenses would be covered as well."

"That sounds better than leaving Sophie with a stranger," Mike mused. "Can I get back to you next week about all this?"

"Registration ends next Friday. Does that give you enough time to make a decision? And to be honest, you don't have to decide about the position until after the training. It paints an accurate picture of what you'd be signing up for. You'll be able to make your decision with your eyes wide open."

"Sounds fair. Thanks for the opportunity, Tom. I'm very interested. As you said though, the training will help me decide for sure."

The men chatted as Mike finished his supper. After a few more patient visits, he headed home. What would Kristen think if he asked her to come to Grand Cayman? Would she assume her presence was simply to watch Sophie? Maybe it was.

Or maybe I would be testing her to see how she and Sophie do together for more than just a few hours, Mike thought. *But that's not right either. It wouldn't be a test. I want her to come because I need her support as I make an important decision. She's part of my life. She needs to be a part of this, too.*

The conference was timed well for Kristen's schedule, he realized. No obstacle there. The obstacles would be in Kristen's mind. He was sure she'd conclude he was using her as a surrogate mother for Sophie. He'd have to convince her otherwise.

Home at last, Mike decided to run the Grand Cayman trip by Anita. He'd learned hard and fast if he didn't keep Anita informed about anything affecting Sophie, he'd pay dearly. But Anita also had a right to know Sophie would be leaving the country, and that she would be under Kristen's care if things worked out. He remembered Sophie had a passport from a trip two years ago to Canada with his parents. So that hurdle was taken care of. Maybe it was a good omen.

Anita answered with caution, obviously seeing Mike's name on the caller ID. "Anything wrong, Mike?" she asked. "It's not like you to call when Sophie's with us here in Indy."

"Nothing's wrong," he answered, trying to keep cool. Anita still had the ability to rattle him. Perhaps that was his fault, though. His guilt about the divorce still played havoc with his thinking when he talked to Anita. It could be her question about something being wrong was just her being a friend.

"I've been offered an intriguing position at the hospital, as chief medical officer," he continued. "It will mean better hours, no weekends, but challenges of a different sort. Anyway, there's a training conference in Grand Cayman that will help me decide about the job. The perk is I get to bring Sophie and a caregiver along. I wanted to get your input before I accepted."

Anita paused, turning Mike's question over in her mind, a practice Mike knew well. She never responded in the moment, always processing information thoroughly before she gave her opinion. It worked for Anita, but the person waiting for an answer was kept on pins and needles.

"It sounds like a wonderful opportunity, Mike. What you haven't said, modest as always, is that it's a credit to your work at Gordon Memorial. I'm proud and happy for you."

"Thanks, Anita," Mike said, stunned at her generous praise. "The conference would end before Sophie starts school. Are you okay with her coming with me?"

Anita laughed, and again Mike felt defensive. "I'm fine with Sophie coming, Mike. But you've left an important piece of information out. Who will be her caregiver, as if I didn't know?"

"I plan to ask Kristen. You've guessed that, obviously. She and Sophie get along well, and I would be out of meetings by early afternoon. Sophie would see plenty of me – she wouldn't be solely with Kristen during the trip."

"Yes, I assumed Kristen would watch Sophie. It wasn't too much of a stretch. Your mother wouldn't be able to handle Sophie alone. But what does this mean for you and Kristen? Things sound serious if you're traveling out of the country with her and Sophie. She means a lot to you, Mike, and I'm glad for you both."

"Kristen hasn't agreed yet, since I haven't asked her. I wanted to talk to you first, as Sophie's mother. I'm relieved to hear you're good with Sophie going on the trip. As for Kristen and me, I'm not sure where we stand. We care for each other, but we get stuck in the particulars of what the future should look like." Mike stopped, unwilling to let Anita in on his concerns about Kristen's profession as a psychologist. He was even less willing to let Anita know of Kristen's reaction to his vision of marriage.

"My guess is you've laid down some rather dogmatic ideas about the perfect wife," Anita said. Her tone was gentle, not mocking. "Kristen's a good woman, Mike. She's smart, capable, and loves our daughter. You'd be wise to let her be the person she is, not some idealized woman whose characteristics are impossible to achieve."

"Point taken. Anita, you're a good friend. I'm grateful to God for that. I'll let you know all the details about the trip as soon as I have them. Tell Grant I said hi. And Sophie too, though my hunch is she's asleep since we've been able to talk this long without interruption."

"Right. Sophie had a busy day. We shopped for school supplies and uniforms. She's actually grown two sizes! And her behavior was stellar. She stayed with me the whole time, which was a blessing since the mall was crazy busy. Have a good evening, Mike."

Since it was still early enough for Kristen to be up, Mike decided to bite the bullet and call her about the Cayman trip. She answered quickly, out of breath.

"Bad time?" Mike asked. "You sound winded."

"Not winded, just avoiding a hot glue drip. What's up?"

"I have an unusual proposition. It involves a free vacation, some light work tending to a certain six-year-old, and lots of sun and seafood. Interested?" Mike's banter masked his fear of Kristen's rejection.

"I'm willing to hear more. Am I going on this 'vacation' as a babysitter, friend, or what?"

Mike explained his conversation with Dr. Wilson, emphasizing the chance for Kristen to relax before her busy fall season started. He minimized his potential promotion, saying only that the conference in Grand Cayman would allow him to assess the new role.

"I see, I think. I'm going as a nanny for Sophie while you decide about your professional future. I'm the babysitter and you're the medical star. Sounds like the last argument we had, doesn't it?"

"It only sounds like that if you interpret it that way," Mike countered. "I really want you to come, Kristen. I'll ask Anita to watch Sophie that week, if you want. We'll have separate rooms, whether Sophie's there or not. I'd rather not make the CMO decision on my own. Your opinion is valuable to me. I've certainly given you lots of advice about your work life, and I'd appreciate yours about mine as well."

Kristen responded with a long stretch of silence. Mike thought the call had been dropped. She was reacting just like Anita – digesting information before she made a decision. Or maybe she was counting to ten before she lost her cool.

"Are you there, Kristen? Hello?"

"I'm here. Trying to get over myself, as usual. I'd be happy to come, Mike. And Sophie can come as well. She'd thrive on a beach vacation. I've got to have faith you're sincere about wanting my opinion. The rules of karma would say 'I've got to trust if I want to be trusted.' Right?"

Unsure of what she meant, Mike decided to agree. "Right. I guess my world view would say trusting God helps things work out the way they should. And I've been reminded lately I'm a little rigid in my views about relationships and marriage. For that, I'm truly sorry."

"Me, too," Kristen said. "I've been comparing you to Rob, unjustly. He was nothing like you. Maybe God is helping us both with our blind spots."

Ten days later, following a rainy flight from Indianapolis, the plane transfer in Atlanta went smoothly. Thankfully, Sophie was able to watch television on the long flight to the Cayman Islands. She enjoyed choosing her beverage and snack from the offerings, eventually settling into a nap before they landed. Kristen spent the flight time reading about Georgetown, the capital city. While Sophie slept, Kristen teased Mike.

"It says here Georgetown has several jewelry stores, with duty-free pricing on luxury items. I think more than meals and a plane ticket should reward my expertise in 'Sophie-care.' Diamond stud earrings would do nicely. A carat minimum, per stone."

"I'm sure they would do nicely," Mike said. "Are you saying you feel taken advantage of? I can pay you hourly if you want." Again, like Anita, Kristen always kept him guessing.

"Chill, would you?" Kristen shot back. "I'm happy to be here. I'm also happy to help with expenses if the hospital won't cover my stay. We could bill them for the earrings, though, right?"

Mike laughed, enjoying the conversation. Kristen's eyes were alight with anticipation. She'd told him this was her first overseas trip, except for an honors biology tour to Costa Rica when she was a senior in high school. She had also informed him she would need some private time during the week to explore Caribbean crafts. Good grief, she would turn this into a regular work week if he didn't intervene.

"In addition to your private time, we also need time to ourselves," he added. "There's a sitting service at the conference hotel each afternoon and evening. Sophie was excited when I told her about it. She said she'd need some time with kids her own age. That child is sharp, as you said to me once when we'd just met."

"Time for the two of us?" Kristen asked. "What did you have in mind? Snorkeling? Looking for shells on the beach? Stingray City?"

"I was thinking an elegant dinner at a restaurant without a children's menu. Maybe watching the sunset to see the mysterious green fire. And also, maybe some cuddling in the dark. I've missed you, Kristen."

Kristen seemed surprised by his serious tone. "I've missed you, too. Or, I've missed what we might become. We had a promising start, but we're off track. In my periods of deep analysis, I've decided we're both afraid. It would be easy to say I'm scared of getting hurt again. But the truth is, I'm afraid of not meeting your expectations. And of what I'd become if my primary goal in life was to please you at the expense of everything else. I won't lose myself for a man ever again."

Kristen's eyes filled. She was telling him the truth. It hurt him to his core to think this beautiful, accomplished woman could be frightened of his judgment. His quest for the perfect woman could cost him that very thing. She was sitting right beside him.

"I would never expect you to please me at all costs, Kristen. You have to believe that. I was, or maybe I am still, afraid. Afraid of another failure, another piece of damage to Sophie's security, another deadened heart. But my fear is mostly behind me now. I believe we could be magic together. And I can't believe I just said that." Mike shook his head. *Magic? Really?*

"Thanks for telling me," Kristen whispered. "So, we're not afraid, we're grown-ups, and we're on an exotic, beautiful island for a week. I'm prepared for some romance!"

The Grand Cayman immigration and customs were a breeze, except when Sophie wanted to pet the drug-sniffing dogs. The ride to the condo complex was smooth, with the ocean, palm trees, and cars enchanting Sophie. She was quick to notice the vehicles had the steering wheel on the "wrong side." Mike explained carefully the need for her to hold his hand when she crossed the street, because traffic patterns were also opposite from what she was used to.

"I'll remember, Daddy," Sophie said solemnly. "I learned in kindergarten about different cultures. This is one, right?"

"Right, honey. It's a British island, so lots of our culture comes from theirs. But some things are different, so be extra careful."

Kristen smiled at the two as they chattered. "Some things cross most cultures," she noted. "Like a daddy's love for his little girl."

"And a mommy's love too," Sophie chimed in. "My mommy loves me, but she also said my heart is big enough to love two mommies. I think she meant you, Kristen."

Kristen and Mike stared at the tiny girl while the cab driver choked on his coffee.

Great, Mike thought. *Sophie's got us married already. We're here for my job training, not a honeymoon. I'd be sure leave Sophie at home if I ever honeymooned with Kristen. And what was Anita's point? She seemed to be giving Kristen her blessing. That's a shocker.*

The cab pulled up to the condo building. Just a few steps from the headquarters hotel, its quarters varied from two-bedroom, two-bath units to five-bedroom, four-bath apartments. The nightly rate for their three-bedroom flat was astronomical, but Mike figured the investment was worth it. He'd take the hospital per diem payment and supplement the rest with his own funds. There was no way the three of them could be content in a standard hotel room. Facing the beach, the condo unit also had a private balcony and full kitchen. Mike didn't expect Kristen to cook, but a fridge and microwave would help with Sophie's need for easy, accessible food.

"This place is gorgeous," Kristen marveled as she walked into the spacious living room. "My bedroom is bigger than my backyard at home. Sophie's is the same. And the master suite, Dr. Sutliff, is worthy of a CMO."

"We'll see," Mike said. "I haven't really learned what the job will entail. But for now, let's enjoy our luxury living. There's a grocery store across the street. Let's get Sophie some snacks and basic food items. I'll be eating lunch at the conference most days."

As with the rest of the island, Foster's grocery store was just British enough to entrance the Hoosiers from Indiana. Along with the usual grocery faire and a large cafeteria take-out line, native eggs (likely from the chickens guarding the store entrance), exotic produce, and magazines from Europe were on offer.

Sophie could barely allow herself to enter the store. "I'm sure the chickens want me to pet them," she announced. "They seem lonely."

"I'm sure they *don't* want you to pet them," Mike said. "They look tame, but they're not. You might get pecked, sweetie."

"Let's choose some food you like so that we can eat while Daddy's at his meeting," Kristen suggested. "We'll each pick one healthy thing, then we'll each pick one dessert."

This plan fooled Sophie for about twenty seconds. "Wait, Kristen. You keep picking healthy things for both of your choices." Sophie's icy eyes glinted, but she was having fun.

"What? You told me you liked cereal for breakfast, so I got

granola. You said you liked blueberries, and I added angel food cake. They'll be terrific together." Kristen was all innocence as she described the dessert.

"My Oreos will be better," Sophie said. "My mommy said to be good for you, so I can eat the angel cake, too."

My girls are a hoot together, Mike thought. *My girls? I think my heart just grew a size or two – like the Grinch. Must be the tropical sun. Or I'm in deeper than I realize.*

After loading their cart, the three Indiana visitors made their way back to the condo. As predicted by the unit manager the cart fit nicely into the elevator, and their food was unloaded into their kitchen with ease. The manager had assured them the cart could be left on the outside walk, to be picked up by grocery store staff after dark.

"That's sure not like home," Sophie said. "We have to bring the cart back to the cart corral and drive home. This is more fun."

They had a quick snack before changing into swimsuits for their first walk on the beach. The white Cayman sand was another revelation to Sophie, who was used to the brown lake sand of Indiana.

"It looks like sugar," she said, scooping the sand and letting it drift through her fingers. "And it's so smooth. I want to make a castle. Did you bring the toys, Daddy?"

Mike took out the sand molds and was ready to dig when Kristen called a halt to the fun. "No playing until we're protected from this sun," she pontificated. "I've been burned enough for ten people in this lifetime, and I don't want to add to it. You two, despite your dark hair, are very fair. Your blue eyes give you away. Come here, Sophie, and I'll 'goop you up,' as my mom used to say."

Mike watched as Kristen spread the SPF 50 over Sophie's little body. "What about me?" he asked. "Who's going to 'goop up' my back?" He hoped Kristen would volunteer. The thought of her hands on his back was very enticing.

"I will, I will," Sophie yelled. "I want to help you, Daddy."

Mike's disappointment must have shown, because Kristen grinned. "Who's going to do my back?" she asked.

"My turn," Mike said quickly, before Sophie could take the task away from him. As he spread the lotion on Kristen's back, he again thought about what a wonderful person she was. Sexy, alluring and all that, but also smart and loving. What was taking him so long? He had to tell her what she meant to him. There would be no better time than this trip. He was determined to get it right this time. Or perhaps he didn't have to focus on getting it completely right, just on telling her the truth about his feelings and trusting the process after that. Wow, he was sounding more and more like the marriage counselor he and Anita had seen in their unsuccessful attempt to save their marriage. Time and maturity had changed him – he hoped.

"Gooping" completed, Kristen sunned herself while Mike and Sophie worked on their castle. As he turned the turret mold over, Mike looked at Kristen.

"What's your pleasure for dinner tonight? We're spoiled for choice. Fast food, pizza, and gourmet restaurants are all close. You get to pick since you're our guest."

Sophie agreed. "Yes, you're the guest, and since you also need to watch me while Daddy's at work, you can pick. But tomorrow I'll pick, okay?"

"Sure, honey, you can choose all you want after today. Since we didn't have a real lunch, and since breakfast was several hours ago, I think we need a substantive supper. Edoardo's across the street has everything from homemade pasta, to fresh seafood, to pizza. Would that work for you two?"

Mike smiled at Kristen in appreciation. She'd obviously studied more than jewelry in the Cayman magazine they'd picked up at the Atlanta airport. She was doing her best to care for Sophie already; she wanted to be sure Sophie wouldn't be hungry after the long day of travel.

"Yum," Sophie said. "I am a little hungry. Maybe after this castle is finished, we can get ready to eat."

Mike again marveled at Kristen's knowledge of his daughter. Kristen knew Sophie was so excited she'd forget she was famished without the little reminder of Edoardo's menu items.

Edoardo's was everything they'd hoped. Kristen and Mike enjoyed the pasta while Sophie sampled gourmet cheese pizza. Their waiter insisted on calling Mike and Kristen "Mama and Papa" much to Sophie's delight. The quick walk back to the condo was made in contented silence.

After her bath and prayers, Sophie fell asleep quickly, without her usual fuss. Mike and Kristen sat on the balcony, sipping the sparkling water they'd bought at Foster's. Reaching for her hand, Mike looked over at Kristen. He was shocked to see her crying.

"What's wrong, my love?" he asked without thinking. "Are you feeling okay? What can I do to help?"

Kristen waived his concern away, as she drew a sniffled breath. "I'm fine. This day has been wonderful, but the Cayman setting brought back a talk I had with my mother when I visited her."

Mike wondered how to proceed. He didn't want to intrude, but he also wanted to help. "If it's too painful to discuss, I'll understand. But I'm also a good listener if you need one."

"Well, you might as well know what a judgmental woman you're dating," Kristen said with a shrug. "I've been angry for *two years* at my mother's insistence that she and my dad go to Grand Cayman after he completed his chemo and radiation. I thought she was being selfish and inconsiderate of his condition. Then when we talked in Phoenix, she told me it was Dad who wanted to go on the trip, and seeing Cayman was his motivation to get through all the invasive procedures, nausea, vomiting, and so on. She said he forced himself to eat, get a little exercise, and do the other rehab so he could enjoy the ocean. They went snorkeling, saw the stingrays, and had a grand time. He even shopped with Mom, which was never his thing! All these months I'd labeled her as selfish. What kind of a person does that make me?"

"It would seem to make you a loving daughter, one who was scared of losing her father," Mike replied. "I can't believe you're feeling so guilty. It's an honest mistake."

Kristen looked at him. The gentle reflection of the moon showed her gratitude at his comments as her face relaxed and her breathing slowed. After a minute, she smiled and said, "Thanks so much for that, Mike. Your forgiveness, on behalf of my mom, is the best gift you could give me this week. I've been sick with self-condemnation ever since we landed."

Then her usual teasing banter returned. "But wait, did you call me 'your love' when you saw me crying? I'm willing to forget those words if you want to take them back."

"I'd never take them back, although they surprised me. Does it bother you that I'm in love with you? When we disagree, it torments me. I want to make things right, instantly! You know I'm impatient, so that's probably not a surprise to you. You're in my thoughts most of the time. And I'll be honest, most of the appeal of this new job is the time I'd get to spend with you. We could be a true couple, a team who spent our time together and made a life of our own."

"A true couple? A life of our own? What are you saying, Mike?"

Chapter Eleven

Kristen watched Mike as he turned away. She thought he'd just proposed, though with his analytical nature she couldn't be sure. Maybe he was just testing out the pros and cons of their relationship as he spoke.

"I'm saying I love you, Kristen. And I want us to have a life together. It's not about you being Sophie's nanny or substitute mother, although your love for her warms my heart. Could you ever see yourself making a family with us? With me?"

"I think I could," Kristen said softly. "I'm just taken by surprise. Have you decided I'm the Proverbs woman? Your focus on the ideal mate still bothers me a little. No, it bothers me a lot."

"Understandably. I talked to Reverend Taylor on the phone before we left. We covered my grief about my failed marriage, my anger, and my obsession to have the perfect soulmate next time around. I even told him about the Proverbs woman thing."

Sensing his embarrassment, Kristen was gentle. "What did he say?"

"He basically called me out, in a very non-ministerial way," Mike admitted with a wry smile. "I could practically see his eyes rolling over the phone connection. He said to focus on examining myself and my part in the divorce. It was like he had taped conversations between Anita and me. My temper, my hard-headed nature, and my sense of superiority were all things he knew about. Maybe he's had psychological training. He was sure if I did an honest review of my marriage, the right woman would come into my life. I told him about you, and he said I was very lucky."

Kristen laughed. "We're both lucky, in my opinion. I love you, too, Mike. But I think I'm more scared of a failed marriage than you are. Can I have some time to think about all this? Let's just enjoy our working vacation for now, okay?"

Reflected in the moonlight, Mike's face was serious. "Is there anyone else? Do you need more time to heal from Rob?"

"No," Kristen said. "That's definitely not it. You and Rob are very different men, thank goodness. I need to do what Reverend Taylor suggested to you – I need to examine myself."

"Fair enough." Mike reached for her hand, and Kristen was grateful for his patience. Her indecision surprised her. He was a good man, a good father, a fine physician, and sexier than any man should be. He was open about his past mistakes and what they had cost him. What was going on with her? Why on earth was she hesitating? Something was holding her back, but she couldn't put her finger on it. Her life was so full already. Did she have room for a ready-made family? She was afraid, but of what?

Mike left early for his meeting the next morning. He left a note thanking Kristen for setting out the granola and telling Sophie to listen to Kristen while he was gone. He promised them a surprise when he returned.

"What do you think Daddy means?" Sophie asked after Kristen read her the note, which was scribbled in true illegible physician fashion.

"I have no idea, honey. In the meantime, let's finish breakfast, goop up, and enjoy the pool. Okay?" Sophie agreed with no argument. Kristen wondered silently how long the good behavior would last.

The pool was almost empty when they arrived a little after ten. Kristen and Sophie set up a card game after taking a quick dip. Only one other family, obviously speaking Italian, was poolside. They were camped directly opposite them. The father was long and lean, the mother trim and sporting a thong bikini.

Their daughter, a little older than Sophie, wore only her bathing suit bottom.

"Where's the rest of her suit?" Sophie whispered.

"It's common in Europe for girls and women to go topless," Kristen explained. "Different cultures, remember?"

"Can I do it too?"

"No, even though we're here, we'll do what we do when we're home."

"Good," Sophie said, clearly relieved. "I'd feel funny without my top."

"Me too!"

At that point, the father walked by them, speaking to someone on his cell phone while he leered at Kristen. Based on his facial expression and inflection, Kristen knew the conversation was smutty and directed her way.

"He's creepy," Sophie whispered again. "He's looking at us funny."

"Just ignore him. We'll stay here for a little while longer, then we'll go to the beach."

Kristen and Sophie finished their card game and gathered their towels to use on the beach chairs. They traced the sandy path down to the ocean, which sparkled as it reflected the morning sun.

The Italian father followed just slowly enough to seem uninterested. He was still on his phone, laughing at a joke his caller told. Kristen was annoyed but not afraid. They were in public, after all. Lots of people were milling around, playing in the sand, and sunning themselves on lounge chairs.

As they enjoyed the view of the ocean, Kristen pointed out a cruise ship ready to unload passengers for their day in Georgetown. Sophie was puzzled.

"Why would anybody want to shop when they could play on the boat or come to our beach?" she wondered. "Shopping is bo-o-o-ring."

"Some folks love to shop," Kristen said "My mother is one.

She's always on the hunt for something special that none of her friends has."

At that moment, "Mr. Sicilian" (as Kristen had styled him), shaded their chairs. Startled, Sophie hopped onto Kristen's lap. Still speaking on his phone, the man again leered at Kristen, and made a "come here" gesture.

So much for cultural courtesy, Kristen thought. This fool was scaring Sophie, and Kristen would not allow that.

"Basta!" Kristen shouted. "Mia famiglia!" she added, as she pointed to Sophie. Having exhausted her command of the Italian language, she followed up with "Leave us alone!"

Turning away on his heel, the Italian seemed slightly ashamed. Other sunbathers began to clap as he left the beach. One woman, speaking with a German accent said, "Thank you, Miss. He's been like this all week. You're the first to stand up to him."

"Wow, Kristen, you're tough," Sophie said with admiration. "Daddy will be proud of how you told that guy off. I didn't know you knew another language. Did you say I was your family?"

"I don't really know any Italian," Kristen admitted. "Last night at supper the waiter said 'Si, basta' when we declined dessert. It means 'enough.' And I heard the word 'famiglia' in a movie. I did call you my family, because I wanted that guy to be ashamed of the way he was acting in front of a little girl who's important to me."

Eyes shining, Sophie said, "I'd like to be your family. Maybe someday?"

"Maybe," Kristen said. "For now, let's have fun. Now that we're free of the silly man, what's next?"

Looking hurt at Kristen's deflection about being family, Sophie decided a walk on the beach would be fun. She was full of questions about the various shells, the pretty sand, and the numerous activities available. Kristen was careful to steer her away from the jet skis, pointing out that those were for older kids and grownups.

Whining, Sophie challenged Kristen. "Why do you always say

I can't do the fun things? It's boring here. I want to go home. My grandma would have things for me to do."

Kristen knew Sophie was tired and not a little upset by the encounter with the European. And by Kristen's refusal to promise they would be a family someday. Diversion usually worked in such instances, but Sophie could be a tough challenge when she was in a mood. Like now. Out of options, Kristen used her mother's stand-by technique as a last resort.

"Usually when I said I was bored, my mom would suggest I do some chores. That helped me think of things to do on my own. What if I said we should go up to our suite and plan our supper? Your daddy said we'd eat in tonight, before his surprise."

"You know you've got supper planned," Sophie said with a sneer. "I got to pick taco casserole. There are no other chores because the maid comes every day. I know what you're doing, Kristen."

"Another thing my mom used to say was that I was overtired if I couldn't think of anything to do. But I can tell you're not tired." If Mom's threat of chores didn't work, she'd try reverse psychology, a stale but effective technique.

"I'm not tired at all," Sophie said, following up with a big yawn. "I'm hot on this beach. Let's go back to the pool and sit under an umbrella."

"Good plan," Kristen agreed. In no time Sophie was asleep in the chair, shielded by the umbrella from the midday sun. Suddenly darkness draped Kristen's chair. Startled and ready to deal with more Italian flirting she sat upright, ready for combat.

"Ouch," Mike said, rubbing his chin where her head hit. "Were you asleep?"

"Not asleep, but drowsy. I thought you were someone else."

"I didn't know you had friends here in Grand Cayman. Who could you possibly know?"

"No one. It's a long story. One of many stories from the short time you've been gone. We should head to the apartment for lunch. Sophie's been stirring. She'll be hungry."

"Whatever you want," Mike said, looking at Kristen with a curious stare.

"Are your meetings over for today?"

"Yes, it's already after one," Mike noted. "If you want some time to yourself after you eat lunch, I can handle Sophie."

"I don't need to be handled," Sophie said, as she rubbed her eyes. "Daddy, Kristen told off a creepy man, and she doesn't want to be in our family even though she said it in his language. She also said I'm too little to be on a jet ski. I want to be with you, Daddy."

Kristen looked at Sophie, paused, and finally had to laugh. "I told you there were stories from today, Mike. I'll explain tonight. How about if you two make our sandwiches while I take a quick walk? I need to clear my head."

"I'll be anxious to hear all about your morning," Mike said. "*Really* anxious. Sophie, let's go make sandwiches and cut up the fruit we bought." The pair left hand-in-hand carrying the towels and beach toys.

What a pair, Kristen thought. *The apple doesn't fall far from the tree. Sophie gets her temper from her dad. What would I be getting into if I married Mike? Would I always be the odd one out? The old psychology truism is that three people make an unstable unit. What if they took turns having temper tantrums?*

Her thoughts were so out of character that Kristen walked almost a mile before realizing she had to get back for lunch. *What happened to my carefree attitude that things always work out?*

Returning to the condo thirty minutes later, she found Sophie in Mike's lap, tearfully talking about the Italian family, with emphasis on the daughter's topless bathing suit.

"Kristen said it's their culture, but we do our own culture even though we're here. I was glad I didn't have to just wear my bottoms."

Mike looked even more perplexed, looking at Kristen for an explanation.

"Sophie's right, Mike. The daughter had her topless look going strong, which bothered Sophie a little. And the dad was creepy. He was on his phone, obviously intent on making us uncomfortable, but he was nothing to worry about. After I told him to scoot, he took off."

"Kristen yelled at him, like the waiter last night," Sophie said. "In his own language, Daddy. It was pretty cool."

Now totally unable to understand anything about the morning, Mike gave up. "Let's eat, girls. I'll get the full story later. Kristen, I trust you if you say this guy's not a problem. I'd be glad to complain to the condo management if you want."

"No need," Kristen said, biting into her ham and cheese sandwich. "I've handled much worse."

"Which is one of my fears about your job," Mike shot back.

Kristen glared, refusing to respond in front of Sophie. "How's your special Cayman almond butter sandwich, Sophie?"

"It's good, but I like peanut butter more. The jelly helps. I'm glad we bought that."

"It's actually fruit preserves, with no added sugar," Kristen said, giving Mike a superior look. "We're eating healthy while we vacation, right?"

"You bet. I yield to you both. My almond butter is wonderful, as are the preserves. I also want to thank you in person for the granola this morning, Kristen. The continental breakfast at the meeting consisted only of cinnamon rolls and coffee. Not much nutrition there."

"You're welcome. Your note also mentioned a surprise?"

Sophie perked up, her mouth full of an apple slice. "What's the surprise, Daddy?"

"I thought tomorrow we could have a special dinner. There's a restaurant that serves great food, has a waterfront dining area with sunset views, and here's the surprise. After dinner you get to feed the tarpon that swim up to the dock."

"What's a tarpon? Is it like a dog?" Sophie continued to crunch her apple, almost daring Kristen to comment on the rudeness of talking with a mouth full of food. She knew better than to fall into Sophie's trap, yet at the same time she had a grudging understanding for Sophie's confusion about the events of the morning.

"A tarpon is a huge silvery fish, taller than I am," Mike said. "They can grow up to eight feet long. They're fun to watch, but I've never been swimming close to them. I think I'd be scared. They look a little like sharks."

"We have to wait until tomorrow to feed the fish?" Sophie asked, still cranky after the trying morning. "Today is still boring." Kristen looked at Mike. Her duties were over for today. He could deal with his daughter. Sophie needed a long nap, but Kristen wasn't going to play bad cop. Mike could figure it out.

"I'm going to walk over to the strip mall next to Foster's while you two enjoy your afternoon together," Kristen announced. "I need to look for gifts for my family and Lauren's baby."

"We're not her family, but she's getting gifts for some baby," a tearful, exhausted Sophie said. "I hate this place."

Mike finally got the picture. "Young lady, it's time for a nap. I'm tired from my meetings, so we'll rest while Kristen is gone." Before she could protest, he picked Sophie up and carried her to her bedroom. After a few minutes he returned with a triumphant look.

"She's out cold," he said to Kristen. "Are you going to be okay? Anything I should know about this morning?"

"Everything is fine," Kristen said, using a phrase she kept in reserve for times she didn't want to talk. "I'll see you and Sophie around four. I'll get dinner started in plenty of time."

Mike took Kristen by her shoulders, gently massaging her tight muscles. "Don't worry about dinner. Don't worry at all. Something's got my girls all upset, and you won't tell me what it is. This trip is supposed to be fun, not stressful." He leaned in, brushing her lips lightly at first, then with more firmness. Kristen responded, wrapping her arms around him.

Breaking away, she asked, "Your girls?"

"That's how I've started thinking of you and Sophie. I love

you both. But my love for you isn't as a nanny or baby mama, which I think is your major fear. I love you for your courage, your intelligence, and that crazy curly hair of yours. This island humidity makes it even sexier."

"That's a new spin on my hair," Kristen noted. "Hard to believe someone would think my Shirley Temple 'do' would be sexy."

"Not just your hair, all of you," Mike said with a wink. "Now go ahead and shop. We'll be fine. I sense you need a break from the Sutliff clan."

Truer words never spoken, Kristen thought as she crossed the busy street to the mall. Mike and Sophie were too intense for her to take right now. Maybe it wasn't them. Maybe it was her.

Am I ready for all of this? For a ready-made family and a man with the highest expectations in a wife? What if I get fat? Or pick foods with additives and preservatives? What if Sophie hates me when she's a teenager? There were too many scary possibilities.

Retail therapy turned out to be just the thing. As she shopped Kristen focused on the island offerings. She bought her mother and sister crushable sun hats with printed scarf bands featuring starfish. Lauren's baby would receive a wall hanging with a grinning cartoon crab. Content, Kristen wandered over to Foster's.

British magazines were stacked in each aisle. Most were full of breathless discussions of the latest controversies surrounding the Royal Family. Kristen shook her head. *Those Royals seem so enmeshed and territorial, and here I'm worried about marrying Mike, a perfectly wonderful man. His parents are darling, and his daughter is a doll. When she's rested, that is. Even his x-wife has given her seal of approval. What more could I want? And what's with my crazy thinking? One minute Mike's a villain, and the next he's God's gift to women.*

She walked into the condo quietly, careful not to awaken Sophie. Mike was on the outside balcony, sipping an iced tea and enjoying the view. She got her own drink and joined him.

"How was your shopping?" he asked. "What did you get me?"

"Shopping was just what I needed. You sound like your daughter, though. I bought hats for my mom and Katie, and a nursery hanging for the Dawson baby. That's it."

"I was kidding. Speaking of Sophie, I need to hear about your morning. She was pretty upset, alternating between admiring your foreign language skills and feeling you'd let her down. What happened?"

Kristen told Mike about the randy man, her use of restaurant/movie Italian, and the applause of the others on the beach. She felt exhausted all over again as she told the story. She glanced at Mike and then punched his arm as she realized he was laughing.

"Not funny," she said. "Well, maybe it is in hindsight, but at the time it was very annoying. There's more."

Now Mike was serious. "What else?"

"I called Sophie 'my family' in Italian. She picked up on it. She asked if we were family, and I hedged. She's sharp enough to sense my hesitation. That explains her grumpy mood. I hurt her feelings, and I don't know what to do."

"Easy. Just say you'll marry me. Marry us. She'd be thrilled, and so would her father." Mike looked at Kristen and took her hand.

I've got to be honest, she thought. *It's time to quit playing around. Time for the hard questions.*

"I love you, Mike," she said. "For a while now, actually. But I'm afraid of your expectations. You're still into that Proverbs woman, which I think is a mask for your own perfectionism and high standards. What if I don't measure up? What if my career doesn't suit your idea of an appropriate job? What if Sophie can't tolerate a stepmom when she's a teen? It's a lot to take on."

Mike seemed to consider her fears. "Honey, you'll always measure up in my book. But I understand your qualms about us Sutliffs. Of course Sophie will have times when you're the wicked stepmom! It's normal, right? And while I hate to admit it, I'll probably still lose my temper on occasion. At which times, it will be only fair that you call me out. Just don't run away, okay?"

She paused, remembering Dr. Cheaney's advice about having the courage to confront even those you cared about. She had to continue – Mike's words were full of love, but they avoided the whole career controversy. "I love my work, too, just as you do yours. My teaching, crafts, and private practice may seem trivial to you, but they're mine. I help people while being creative. Most folks never find a career niche like that. You don't understand how important it all is to me."

Mike studied her with a surprising sadness in his eyes. "I've done what I swore I'd never do. I promised myself I'd never hold another woman to impossible standards, which is what I did with Anita. I couldn't understand why she wasn't content to be home with Sophie. The place was a mess, meals were microwaved, and I thought it was her being lazy. She was depressed and lonely, which the marriage counselor tried to tell me. I just couldn't hear it. I hated that our marriage was dying with little Sophie in the middle. I made it Anita's fault."

"Have you told Anita this?" Kristen asked. "She needs to hear it, and you need to say it to her. My sense is she'd be a lot easier for you to deal with if you were open."

"You're right. I need to do it intentionally. I always hope we'll have time during the drop-offs and pick-ups, but of course we don't."

Mike sipped his tea and went on. "But back to my original statement. I resolved not to hold any other woman to unrealistic standards, but I've done it to you. Your careers are crucial to you, and therefore they are to me, too. I'll be honest, though. When you see patients alone in the office at night, I do worry."

"I get that. Once Lauren is back from maternity leave, we'll arrange our schedules so we both work the same evenings. Even if one of us doesn't have a patient to see, there's always paperwork to do. Would that help?"

"It would," Mike said with a smile. "That said, I'll ask again. Kristen, will you marry me? I love you. Sophie loves you. We'd be terrific together."

After hesitating for a nanosecond, Kristen knew what to do. Things were finally clear – Mike's sincere devotion, Sophie's six-year-old brand of possessive love, and Kristen's own realization that her life would be empty without the two demanding Sutliffs. What kind of faith did she have – in God, in the world, in herself – if she couldn't take a chance on loving this pair?

"I will," Kristen said. "You and Sophie are worth the risk. But beware, I'm going to stand up for myself, Mike. Got it?"

"I've got it, for sure," Mike said. "Now for the fun stuff. After all, relationships aren't just about verbal communication."

The rest of the afternoon was spent kissing and holding hands on the balcony lounge while Sophie slept.

Thank goodness for a kid who naps! Kristen thought. *If I'm going to marry this man, we're going to need some time alone!*

Chapter Twelve

After an uneventful morning by the pool and beach, Kristen and Sophie met Mike for a late lunch in the condo. Today's meal was "leftover smorgasbord," with Kristen and Mike having taco casserole while Sophie stuck with her almond butter sandwich. Naps for everyone followed in anticipation of a fine dinner. Sophie was in a better mood and announced, "I won't be afraid of the *tarpooons*. I'm tough like Kristen."

The taxi ride to the restaurant was brief. Mike decided it was time to tell Sophie about his and Kristen's engagement.

Thank you, God, for my two girls. Let me be a better husband and father than in the past, he thought, as the waiter led them to their beachside table.

After drinks were ordered, Mike spoke. "Sophie, what would you say about you, me, and Kristen becoming a family?"

Sophie's face scrunched in concern. "She may not want to, Daddy. Yesterday she only said 'maybe' when I asked her."

"I thought about it, honey," Kristen said. "I love your daddy and you so much it was foolish of me to hesitate. But now I'm sure."

"That's GREAT!" Sophie shouted, spilling the water at her side and alarming the sedate clientele. "But where's your ring? You can't get married without a ring."

"That's our next job," Mike said smoothly. "There are lots of jewelers in Georgetown. My conference has childcare available in the afternoons, so I thought Kristen and I could shop tomorrow while you played with kids your own age for a few hours. What do you say?"

"I say okay, but not every day. I like being with Kristen, and she can keep the silly man away from us."

Everyone laughed and proceeded to enjoy their meal. Sophie settled on grilled cheese, but Mike and Kristen made the most of the fresh seafood highlighted on the menu. Feeding the tarpons, as they lunged at snippets of bread and swirled in the water, was almost anticlimactic after the eventful dinner. Sophie was tired in the taxi and went to bed immediately after their return to the condo.

"Think she'll be this good when we have her for your custody visits?" Kristen asked as they made their way to the balcony. "This seems like a stepchild honeymoon."

"I agree," Mike said, following it up with a kiss. "But I'll take it for now."

He marveled that Kristen had agreed to marry him after resisting for so long. Not that he'd made it easy. His antiquated search for the ideal partner had nearly derailed his chance at love with such a wonderful woman. She was beautiful inside and out. Her sun-kissed skin and lightened hair added to his attraction, but then she'd been beautiful to him in cloudy Indiana as well. He was a lucky guy.

"Well, what made my case with you?" he continued. "I was planning to propose at least three more times before you said yes."

"My shopping trip did the trick," Kristen said, with mock sincerity. "I figured my meager budget would be much healthier if I married a doctor who's also chief of staff."

"Ah, now I see," he needled back. "About the new position – I'm enjoying what I've learned this week. The administrative work suits me, or at least it does when we do simulated case studies in our meetings. I'll also be able to practice medicine part-time and have responsibility for one wing of the smaller floor in the hospital. I'm going to take the job, but as my future wife, you should have some input, too. What do you think?"

"I think it's a good fit," Kristen said. "You've been enthused after each session. You won't have to work seven twelve-hour shifts anymore. You'll get weekends off. I think Sophie will benefit, too. Your parents are aging, and they should enjoy their health while it lasts. Sophie can be a handful, as we know."

Yes, he knew. Sophie was part of his package, and he again thanked God for Kristen's acceptance and love of his little girl. Sophie was a child of divorce, but she was deeply loved by Grant and Kristen. Not many kids with divorced parents were that fortunate.

"True. Mom has said she wants to do some traveling, but I've needed her and Dad to cover with Sophie. The freedom will be good for them, too. Speaking of health, how's your mother?" Mike had been so absorbed with his proposal to Kirsten he'd forgotten about Kaye's illness.

"Katie emailed and said she's better. She's following the no-added-sugar diet and doing pool aerobics. The mood swings and outrageous plans for marriage have disappeared. Could managing blood sugar have such a drastic effect?"

"Possibly," Mike said slowly. "Your mom's always been somewhat flighty, right? That part of her personality will still be there, but hopefully not with such drastic behavior. So, you're going to be the only bride in the family for a while?"

"Very funny. Unless Katie's new man is more serious than she is, I should have center stage. Which brings me to the topic of ring shopping. What did you have in mind? What's our budget?"

Kristen said the words lightly, though Mike sensed she was being cautious about money. He smiled at the woman he loved so much. Despite her tone, her eyes were serious as she asked about the ring. Her butterscotch tan and bleached out ringlets kept adding to her appeal. She was ravishing.

"If you keep wearing that bikini from early in the week, the budget is unlimited," he said, with a meaningful stare.

"That bikini got me into trouble with the Italian guy," Kristen said. "It's going to be one-piece suits for me for the rest of the trip."

"Then a wedding band it is," Mike replied. "Maybe on our

twentieth anniversary you can have a ring with a diamond chip set in it."

"Okay," Kristen said, playing along. "Maybe I'll talk to 'Mr. Sicilian' about getting cozy. Of course, Sophie would tell on me."

Mike laughed at Kristen's banter. To her credit, she hadn't complained about watching Sophie or about all the work involved. Even in their good times Anita wouldn't have tolerated such a vacation. Sophie's temperament had always been a mismatch for Anita's, but they seemed to be growing closer as Sophie matured a little. *Fingers crossed,* he thought. *Kristen would be a great stepmom, but a girl still needed her mother.*

"Kristen, you're the best. Thanks for your sense of humor and for all you've done for Sophie. To get back to your original question, I have no idea what jewelry costs. We'll play it by ear tomorrow. One thing strikes me though. I'd like your ring to have stones that remind us of this trip. It's been a piece of heaven for me."

"Hmmm. That could open up your wallet more than you think, Mike. The magazine from the airport is full of jewelry ads. Sapphires, tanzanites, and diamonds are pricey."

"It will work out," Mike said as he nuzzled Kristen's ear. "You always used to say that, remember?"

"So I did," Kristen reflected. "I'm believing it more each day."

Mike found himself distracted during the next morning's meetings. What kind of ring would Kristen want? Anita had made do with his mother's ring, although it was no sacrifice. Jane Sutliff's large rose-cut diamond, set in an antique mounting, had suited Anita well. He'd allowed her to keep it after the divorce due to his guilt. Maybe that had been a mistake.

No, Kristen deserved a new ring, and he was making a fresh start. It was time to enjoy all a fresh start entailed, ring shopping included.

Sophie had lunch at the childcare center next to the conference hotel, so Mike and Kristen were able to enjoy their meal by the pier in Georgetown.

"Time to warm up your credit card, Dr. Sutliff," Kristen said, as she stood to leave the restaurant. "I'm in the mood for a flashy piece of jewelry."

"I'm ready," he said, grabbing her hand. "Let's go break the bank."

This should be interesting, he thought. A hefty purchase would be the first test of how they dealt with challenges as a couple. Gulping, he led Kristen into a large jewelry store.

"How may I help you?" the salesman asked. Introducing himself as Nigel, his British accent was heavy, with an obvious attempt at an aristocratic tone. He wore a tailored suit, complete with a vest, and had a pocket square to coordinate with his bowtie. Between the upper-crust accent and the custom clothes, Mike thought he was laying it on a little thick.

"We'd like to look at engagement rings," Mike said. "Something with meaning to remind us of our trip."

Before the man could pull out the first tray of rings, Kristen called out from one aisle over. "Mike, look at these. They're beautiful."

"Ah, the canary diamond collection," Nigel said with a swoon. "Those would be lovely with your hair, miss. They also bring to mind the Cayman sunsets."

Oh brother, Mike thought. *This guy is a pro.*

Kristen must have also sensed an overselling moment and took charge.

"Nigel, I've read that fancy light yellow diamonds are less expensive than the deeper hues. Let's look at those."

Nigel seemed underwhelmed by Kristen's knowledge. "Well, miss, you're correct. The fancy light shades are more economical. Better yet, in terms of cost, are the honey-yellows, like these in the pink case."

"Oh, I love this one," Kristen said, pointing to a diamond the exact shade of her sun-bleached curls. "It's just like the sunset from the balcony."

"And like your hair," Mike said. "What can you do for us on this piece, Nigel?"

Nigel sniffed, showing his distaste for negotiation. "This diamond, although not the highest quality or color, is beautiful on the lady's finger. It weighs 1.4 carats, is very well cut for a pear shape, and has distinctive fire."

"Just like the lady," Mike said with his characteristic grin. "How much?"

After hedging about the added value of the white diamonds on each shoulder of the teardrop stone, Nigel quoted a price ten percent less than the tag. Mike accepted the offer.

The ring fit Kristen perfectly. Wearing it as they left the store, she said, "Mike, this is more than I expected. Are you sure about the ring?"

"I'm sure about all of it. About you, about our soon-to-be family, and about our future together. If you're wondering, I haven't thought of the Proverbs woman in ages."

"I'm still searching the Bible for the Proverbs man," Kristen said as she eyed her ring. "Surely God had something specific to say about the ideal husband."

I sure hope not, Mike thought. *I may be in big trouble if she finds that reference.*

Later, after fetching Sophie and "gooping up," the trio went to the beach. As Mike and Sophie played a few yards down the beach from Kristen, "Mr. Sicilian" sauntered slowly by. Showing his trademark leer, he launched into a lengthy monologue, obviously aimed at Kristen and her tankini top. His message, complete with hand gestures toward her midsection, was probably that today's bathing suit was too conservative. Before she could warn him off, Mike stood by the man.

"Andiamo," Mike said calmly, with a tight grasp on the man's shoulder. "You're bothering my family, yet again. Beat it."

The pest moved away, cursing in his native language. He

seemed, however, to understand Kristen and Sophie had a protector. The white fingerprints embedded in his suntanned skin no doubt enhanced his awareness. He would move on to other isolated females.

"Daddy, you know Italian too!" Sophie cried. "That was so cool. What did you say?"

"I said, 'let's go' or 'hurry up.' He got the message. After you and Kristen told me about him, I searched online for some Italian words during one of my breaks at the conference. You're lucky I didn't use the bad words I found."

Kristen laughed. "You're a peach, Mike. Despite my protests of independence, it felt good to be rescued." She followed up her thanks with a quick kiss. Mike held her several seconds longer, nuzzling her curls while he enjoyed the scent of coconut "goop."

Sophie wrinkled her nose. "Yuck. I'm going to make more castles. You guys stay here if you're going to get mushy."

Mike thought mushy sounded great, but this wasn't the time or place. He veered instead into planning mode. "What about the wedding? Big, little, fancy, simple? Vegas, Gordon, some island? We have lots to consider."

Kristen hesitated for a beat. "I don't really know. I've got the Fall Fest to prepare for and staff, I've got Lauren's clients to cover, and I'll be teaching a couple of courses soon. What kind of wedding do you want?"

Mike knew her caution was partly due to feeling overwhelmed. But something else was going on with the woman he treasured. He wanted to be honest, though. "Anita and I had a big wedding, with all the tradition and expense you can imagine. This is your first wedding, though, so if you want all that I'm in."

"You mentioned expense. I just can't afford a big production. Mom used the bulk of her inheritance from Dad to buy into the facility in Arizona. They'll care for her for the rest of her life, even if she runs out of funds. Katie and I got a little money. I used mine to help with payments on my house. You're not marrying a pauper, but I have a tiny savings account. Anyway, a small wedding would suit me fine. Timing is a bigger issue."

Mike didn't want to wait until after the holidays to marry Kristen. She was making it sound like January was their only option. Since there wasn't a huge amount of planning to do, it was silly to wait. He tried not to sound pushy.

"Don't you have a fall break at school?" he asked. "After the Fall Fest? We could get married that weekend."

"Maybe," Kristen said, in a tone full of doubt. "A small wedding still involves lots of planning. I'm not sure we could get it all together by then. We need proper clothes, a cake, food, a venue, a minister…"

"My sense is our mothers could handle all that, and more," Mike said. "Isn't your mom coming in for the Fest? Could she come a few weeks early? What about Lauren? She might need a diversion as the baby gets settled. She could help. Do you think she'd design your dress? You've said what a talent she is."

"Maybe," Kristen said again, with the same uncertainty. "I need to take a walk, Mike. Things are closing in. I've only been engaged for a few hours!"

"You're right," he admitted. "I'm sorry for pushing. I just want us to be together. We'll get married when the time is right for both of us."

Kristen looked relieved. She headed down the beach, carefully choosing the opposite direction from the Italian intent on harassing her. Mike watched her with concern.

My, I love that woman, he thought. *She's tough, as Sophie says, but she's also wounded. She's worried about her job, her mother, her friend, and her clients. I've got to give her some space. She should enjoy being a bride, and if she needs time, that's okay.*

"Where did Kristen go?" Sophie asked. "Did you boss her around?"

Mike hooted and picked up his daughter. "You know me well, missy. I did get a little bossy, but I said I was sorry. Okay?"

"Daddy, you keep telling me to think before I speak. You've got to keep a lid on it. Kristen's our family now."

There it was. His six-year-old had a perfect handle on the situation. If he and Kristen were to be a couple, he should treat her as the valued family member she was. Even though they weren't married, she'd shown every motherly characteristic possible to Sophie. She'd also demonstrated her love for him. Her concern about the cost of the ring was telling, too – she was protective about his finances and willing to choose a smaller diamond if needed.

"Sophie, I'm going to get mushy with you," he said, giving her a big smooch on her sandy cheek. "You're one smart cookie."

Kristen returned from her walk dripping with sweat but in a better mood. She kissed Mike, then Sophie. Relieved, Mike asked, "What are our plans for dinner? It's been a big day for all of us, what with us officially becoming a family. Any ideas?"

Sophie said she didn't care but was getting pretty hungry.

"Why don't we walk to Foster's and get takeout from their cafeteria line?" Kristen asked. "They had a huge variety of options, and I noticed some creamy mac 'n cheese that might appeal to a certain someone."

"Yum! I don't want to wait for food to be done. My tummy is growling."

Well, Sophie's eating and gaining a little weight, Mike thought. His eyes glistened in gratitude for Kristen's influence on Sophie's appetite. He also had to remind himself again that Anita had chided him about being too rigid about Sophie's food choices. What a stubborn fool he'd been. In so many areas.

Kristen put her arms around his neck. "You okay? We don't have get takeout if you'd rather not."

"I'm fine," Mike replied. "I'm just counting my blessings and thanking God for you and Sophie." Kissing her soundly, he said, "Let's get cleaned up and head to Foster's. I'm starving, too!"

"Better yet, let me go," Kristen suggested. "I'll take your food orders, and you and Sophie can shower. Then I'll get presentable while you set out the feast."

One hour later, Mike reveled in the simplicity and fun of the meal. Sophie had eaten her mac 'n cheese, along with part of his meatloaf and much of Kristen's chicken and noodles.

That kid is going through a growth spurt, Mike thought. *Anita tried to tell me that, too. Could I be more clueless? Kristen told me to make amends with Anita. And she's right.*

Exhausted from the day's events, and still singing Mike's praises for getting rid of the "creepy man," Sophie went right to bed. Mike returned to the condo living room with a smile.

"The stepchild honeymoon continues," Kristen said. "It's nice to have private time, though. Now that I've thought it through, we need to talk about the wedding. How about Thanksgiving weekend? It will be simple to plan a small ceremony by then. The biggest obstacle will be location. What do you think?"

"I think we need to catch our breath," Mike said, slipping his arms around Kristen. "When we come up for air, we can continue this discussion."

Mike kissed Kristen's temples, her neck, and finally her lips. She groaned slightly but responded to his touch. Several minutes later, she forced them back to reality.

"Back to the issue at hand," she said. "Who's going to perform this ceremony?"

"Reverend Taylor will work us in, I'm sure."

"Even if I don't attend your church?"

"Sure. He's the one who told me I was lucky to have you, remember? You're forgetting bigger challenges. Do you want a church wedding? Or a ceremony somewhere else? And your mom and sister will have to book their flight soon if they want a seat on Thanksgiving weekend."

"You're right. Mike, your attention to detail saves the day once again. To be honest, I've always wanted an outdoor wedding. As a faculty member, I can use the GCC commons over Thanksgiving break for free. And I'll call my mother with our news when we get back to the States. You have to tell your parents also. And Anita."

Noting the concern on Kristen's face, Mike kissed her and replied. "Anita will be fine. She's also reminded me you're a keeper. It speaks volumes when an ex gives her approval to the new woman. Especially if the new woman is to be a stepmother to her daughter."

"Okay, I'm convinced," Kristen said as she leaned back on Mike's lap. "I'm also tired. It's been a day, huh? I've got a new diamond ring, a macho fiancé who speaks Italian, and an 'almost' stepdaughter with a raging appetite. Life is good."

Two days later, the magical trip was over. The flights home were more complex than before. Immigration and customs in Atlanta seemed to take forever since the electronic kiosks were out of commission. Sophie soon tired of the long lines, stuffy air, and loud noises. Mike thought she was close to a meltdown but was at a loss to prevent it.

"Sophie, let's play a game during this long wait," Kristen said. "Want to play 'I spy'?"

"What's that?" Sophie asked, not really interested. "It sounds stupid."

"It's pretty hard. Mostly second-graders play it. Maybe it's too much for you."

"I can do it," Sophie insisted. "Let's play."

Mike was truly grateful for Kristen's ability to engage Sophie. They played their game for the next fifteen minutes, at which point they were ready to recheck their bags and search for some supper. The last leg, from Atlanta to Indianapolis, would be quick. Hopefully Sophie would snooze during the one-hour flight and then again on the drive from Indy to Gordon.

Chicken fingers and fries satisfied Sophie, and Mike's hopes about a quiet trip home were realized. As he drove "his girls" to Gordon, he glanced at Kristen's sleeping face in the seat next to him. She was spent, too. Dealing with his daughter, and him for that matter, was more taxing than he'd realized. He was very lucky to have her, as Reverend Taylor had said.

Chapter Thirteen

Kristen woke up wondering where she was. The late flight from Atlanta and the drive to Gordon seemed ages ago. Was it a dream? She looked at her left hand, realizing with a thrill it was all real. She was engaged to Mike. She had handled parenting chores with Sophie as well. Maybe life did work out after all. Maybe God had a hand in all this. Mike's faith might be more powerful than she'd thought.

Her cell phone played the bubble gum pop song identifying Annie as the caller. *This should be good,* Kristen thought.

When Kristen answered, Annie jumped right in. "So spill, girlfriend," she said between slurps of coffee. "Any steamy nights I should know about? How was the kid? Did Mike get serious? Most importantly, how many lobster dishes did you order?"

Laughing, Kristen answered. "There was some steam, for sure. The 'kid,' whose name is Sophie, was great. She's a sweetheart. I had plenty of seafood, of course. And about the 'serious' question, are you asking if I'm engaged? Because I am!"

Choking sounds filled the other end of the call. "Wait, I swallowed my coffee down the wrong pipe," Annie gasped. "You're engaged? Like with a ring and everything? To the doctor feared by one and all?"

"Quit that," Kristen scolded. "Admit it, you like him better than before. He's really a fine man, and he respects my career. That was my main concern, but he's gotten beyond that."

"Whatever you say. Have you told your mom and Katie? When's the wedding?"

"I've got to call them today. We don't want to wait too long to get married. Maybe Thanksgiving weekend, if we can make it work. You'll be around, right?"

"Kristen, I'd be around no matter when you were getting married. This will be an event second to none! But why wait so long?"

"There's just too much to do. My two online courses start in a week, Lauren's caseload is heavy, and the Fall Fest is in mid-October. I'll have to be a crafting genius to be ready in time."

"Why bother with the Fest?" Annie asked as she chewed on her bagel. After another gulp of coffee, she continued. "You'll be rolling in the bucks when you see all Lauren's clients, not to mention being engaged to a moneybags doctor."

"Funny. As if you'd let a man totally support you."

"I just might. Especially if he looked like Mike. I'd adjust quickly to all that money and hotness."

Kristen knew her friend was joking but had to set her straight. "Again, funny. For your information, Mike pays child support faithfully. Sophie's school tuition is probably going to be in play in a few years. Plus, hospitalists don't make the money specialists do. Mike says the big earners in medicine do out-patient procedures or surgery."

Her voice dripping with sarcasm, Annie said, "Yeah, you'll be clipping coupons for the rest of your life. I'll let you know when the thrift store has its 'fill up a bag for five dollars' sale." The women laughed together.

Then Annie got down to business. "So, do you have a ring? Or did the Cayman Islands lack a sufficient jewelry selection?"

"The selection was wonderful. Nigel gave us a pretty good deal." Kristen waited for the expected response from her funny friend.

"Nigel? Did he have a la-di-da British accent? Was he condescending?"

"Yes, ma'am. Right on all counts. But it's a great memory. And the ring is pretty wonderful, too."

Plans were made to meet for lunch after Kristen saw her morning clients. Annie arranged for her students to work on their care plans in the afternoon and promised to grill Kristen extensively about the Cayman trip details, focusing on the heated ones.

"And I don't mean humidity and air-quality index," she warned Kristen.

Kristen had a one-hour break between patients. She reached her mother, who sounded surprised but pleased at the news about Mike. Kristen was encouraged by her mother's skepticism as well.

"Honey, how come I've never heard about this man? Isn't this a little sudden? Is he a good guy?"

Kaye was being appropriately motherly, and Kristen appreciated it. "Mom, he's the best. It's a little quick, I'll grant you, but I'm sure about Mike. There's another plus for you – you'll have a darling step-granddaughter."

"I'll love her like she's yours," Kaye answered. "You know that!"

Kristen placed a quick call to Katie, who was also thrilled. "I knew you were bluffing when you were in Phoenix. All that talk about 'figuring out if he was worth the time' was baloney. I could tell you were smitten."

"*Smitten?* Have you been reading Jane Austen novels again? You're talking like a Regency heiress."

"I love Jane Austen," Katie huffed. "She was a genius. She also knew about arrogant men. Is Mike okay in that regard? Sometimes doctors are pretty full of themselves."

"He's wonderful, Katie. We've both had to get over ourselves a little, but we're a good team. I've been kicking myself for all the grieving I did over Rob. He wasn't a bad person, but Mike is the best."

"That's good enough for me. I'll call Mom and arrange for plane tickets. We'll do our best to get to Gordon the weekend before Thanksgiving. There will be lots of details we can help you with."

Thank you, God, Kristen thought. *My family is wonderful, a true blessing. Dad will be at my wedding in spirit. I can't believe I'm praying, but hopefully You won't hold any grudges about my previous lack of faith. I'm still learning about trusting You.*

With that silent prayer, Kristen went to the lobby to meet her next patient. Kyle Stamper had been seeing Lauren for a combination of psychotherapy and career counseling. He was a fiftyish engineer, just laid off from his company in a downsizing move.

"What do I do now?" he asked Kristen. "My wife won't leave Gordon, but there are no jobs for me here. The career test I took with Lauren said I have good mechanical skills. Duh - I'm an engineer. Where does that leave me?"

"I reviewed the test results," Kristen answered. "The assessment also showed you have great interpersonal skills, which is sometimes unusual for engineers. Those soft skills could be in high demand when combined with your engineering background. I think we should start with revamping your resume, so you'll stand out from the others who were downsized."

Kyle was skeptical but listened attentively as Kristen outlined the changes she would make to his resume. She booted up her computer, showing Kyle the numerous job search sites online. Careful to caution him she said, "The old adage is that looking for a job is a full-time job, Kyle. You'll probably send many resumes out with no response. The hard part is not taking it personally. It only takes one hit for you to get a good job."

"I'm tenacious. Just ask my wife," he said. "But I'm still not sold on the soft skills stuff. Are you talking about management jobs? Or consulting?"

"We won't know until you comb those job sites. Here's your homework for this week: search the job market online, make a spreadsheet so you can keep track of where you've applied, and rework your resume. It's probable you'll need more than one resume. They should be tailored to specific jobs to have the most impact."

Looking slightly aghast, Kyle shook his head. "When you said looking for a job is a real job, I didn't believe you. Now I do. What about age discrimination? I'm nearly fifty-six, and my gray hair shows it."

"I'd be lying if I said age discrimination didn't exist. Just sell your experience and flexibility and see what happens. Another option would be retraining in a different field, one that needs professionals. Have you ever thought about teaching math or science?"

"My wife suggested that. She said GCC has an intensive teacher-training program for high school STEM classes. Maybe I'll look into that as part of my homework."

"Sounds like an excellent plan," Kristen said. "How are you doing emotionally, Kyle? Losing a job can be devastating." *As I know all too well,* she thought.

"I'm doing fine," Kyle said, setting his jaw. "Lots of my peers have said without a job, they don't know who they are anymore. I know I'm still God's child. My identity doesn't hinge on what I do for a living. God will provide."

The session ended with Kyle promising to return next week with at least three versions of his resume in hand. Kristen marveled at his faith. *Here's a guy supporting two kids in college, whose wife won't move to a bigger city, and he's secure in his belief that God will get him through. I could learn from him. No more berating myself for needing three jobs to support my needs. I know who I am - God's child.*

Annie was at the local cafeteria when Kristen arrived. They went through the line, Annie focusing on starch and sweets, while Kristen chose a salad and fresh fruit.

"Really? You're dieting *after* a beach vacation?" Annie looked at her own turkey and stuffing with a shrug. "I need sustenance. My students are whining up a storm as the summer classes come to a close. Everyone has a different sob story. Carbs are good for my mood. I'm sure I've read that in a professional journal."

"I know you, Annie. You can't fool me. You'll sympathize with all of your students, cutting them breaks if they do lots of remediation. Just be careful – that's what got me into trouble with Heather."

Kristen's faced clouded at the memory. She reminded herself that Heather was in a different place now and had sought out the provost to plead Kristen's case.

"On to more exciting things," Annie said with her mouth full. "Tell me everything about Mike and the trip, especially Mike's loving behavior." Gazing at Kristen's ring, she continued. "If this is an indication of the poverty-stricken life you're about to lead, I'm not convinced. This is a real rock!"

Laughing, the two friends enjoyed their lunch while Kristen described the week in Grand Cayman, including the unpleasant European, ring shopping, and all the delicious seafood. She left out Mike's decision to take the chief's job, uncertain whether it was public knowledge yet.

"All I can say is, does he have a brother?" Annie teased.

"Only child. I'll be on the lookout for cousins, though."

Kristen's phone rang. She was concerned to see Lauren's number on the ID. "What's up, friend? Are you and the baby okay?"

"More than okay," Lauren said, her voice soft and fatigued. "He's lying right next to me. We had quite a night, but he's here and he's healthy. He even broke the six-pound barrier. I'm not sure what I'd have done if I'd carried him to term – the doctor said he'd have weighed over ten pounds!"

Congratulations and tears were shared. Kristen made plans to visit after Lauren was home and settled in with the baby.

"Think that will ever happen for me?" Annie asked after the call ended. Her sad tone was unusual for her.

Kristen comforted her friend. "Of course it will," she said. "My relationship with Mike sure snuck up on me. The same will happen to you."

"Yeah, right. That's what people in love always say to people like me."

Kristen's phone rang again. Since she didn't know the number, she let the call go to voice mail. She and Annie parted – Kristen on her way back to the therapy office; Annie headed to campus to grade the endless care plans submitted by students as part of their final projects.

After an hour of writing case notes and completing insurance forms, Kristen remembered she had a voice mail. The provost's administrative assistant asked Kristen to call Dr. King on his private number as soon as she could.

"Hi, Dr. King," Kristen said tentatively when he picked up. She'd met the provost only once, at a large reception, so she doubted he remembered her. "It's Kristen Anderson, returning your call."

"Hello, Dr. Anderson," he responded. "I've recently learned of the situation with your student Heather, and about the dean's response. Given the supporting information offered by the student, your department chair, and the dean's history, I'd like to reinstate your tenure-track position, beginning this spring. I'm unable to implement it this fall since enrollments are down, but the spring will offer plenty of classes to teach in your area of expertise. If enrollments dip in the future, we'll find research tasks for you to maintain your tenure-track status."

Kristen sat in silence, causing the provost to ask if she were still on the line.

"I'm here, Dr. King. I'm just so surprised. And grateful, of course."

"Dean Benson has had several complaints lodged against him. I can't reveal them since they comprise a personnel matter, but your teaching evaluations and Dr. Stevens's support made it clear GCC needs a faculty member of your caliber. The student involved, Heather Tilson, also made a strong case in your favor, contradicting her initial complaint." The provost's formal manner belied his praise. Kristen couldn't believe her ears.

"Thanks again, Dr. King," Kristen said. "I'm thrilled. GCC is very special to me, as are its students."

Absorbing the impact of the call and wanting to share the good news, Kristen tried to reach Mike. His phone went straight to voice mail, not an uncommon occurrence when he was on the road to Indianapolis to deliver Sophie. She'd tell him her good news tonight.

Just as she finished dinner, Kristen's phone pinged. Mike texted that due to a semi-truck accident, he was stuck in a traffic jam on I70. He promised to call tomorrow, saying cell reception on the highway was iffy at present.

Keep him safe, Kristen prayed. She caught herself, wondering if she was praying correctly. Her prayers were almost always requests of some sort. Maybe she should meet with Reverend Taylor to ask about this stuff.

Her phone rang, chasing her guilty thoughts away. The ID revealed Heather's name.

"Hi, Heather," Kristen said. "Is this an emergency? Are you okay?"

Ragged sobs and shallow breathing answered Kristen's queries. "I'm okay, but I need to see you tomorrow if possible. Cody and I had a big fight. He's being unreasonable about the wedding. Then he said he felt trapped, and he stormed out of the apartment. What am I going to do?"

Kristen felt for the young woman. She'd known Heather's unrealistic expectations of her marriage would catch up to her. "Come in tomorrow at nine, Heather. If possible, bring Cody with you."

"He won't come. I already suggested it," Heather said with a whimper. "He says I have to get myself together, that he's not the one with a problem. It's all on me according to him."

"I'll see you at nine then. In the meantime, let me do my crisis check. Did Cody hurt you? Any thoughts of self-harm? And have you eaten today?"

"No, he would never hit me or anything. I'd never hurt myself either. I have my baby to consider. But you reminded me I haven't eaten since I had a piece of toast for breakfast. I'll make some dinner when we hang up."

"Sounds good, Heather. See you tomorrow." Kristen hung up, hoping Heather and Cody could each be mature enough to solve their differences. Planning a wedding while dealing with an unexpected pregnancy would test the most stable of relationships.

I'm not pregnant, but I'm still overwhelmed by planning my own wedding, she thought. *Give me wisdom when I talk to Heather, dear Lord.*

There she went, asking for favors again when she prayed. Kristen put an alert on her phone to call Reverend Taylor tomorrow. It was time.

Bernie barked, telling his owner he needed an evening walk. Since she'd returned from Grand Cayman, her pooch had been extra demanding.

"Yes, my handsome boy," Kristen said as she ruffled his downy ears. "We both need some exercise. After that, we'll do some crafting."

Following their walk, which resulted in Bernie getting lots of attention from Kristen's neighbors, she focused on building more inventory for the Fall Fest. Annie's comments that Kristen should just let the Fest go were tempting. Kristen couldn't do it, though. She'd made a commitment, paid for booth space, and she wanted to experience the one-on-one interactions with buyers. She was also thinking ahead about wedding expenses. The income from the Fest would help a lot in that area. Wedding dresses were costly.

Kristen surveyed her depleted inventory of craft supplies. She'd added materials a few weekends ago but had used up most of what she had purchased. Her eyes floated to the bag of quilt scraps she had saved from making the stuffed teddy bears. If she could think of ways to use the scraps, she could make even more money.

A quick online search did the trick. Kristen's artistic skill soon resulted in mini tree ornaments, quilt-edged hand towels, eyeglass cases, hot pads, and more. In a few hours' time she had twenty-five items, which could be priced at a few dollars each.

Way to go, she encouraged herself. *Maybe Mike's nameplate was on target. I do have artisan sensibilities!*

A knock at the door caused Bernie's usual ferocious barking. Kristen released the deadbolt to see Mike on her porch. He greeted her with a kiss.

"What's up?" Kristen asked. "I thought you were stuck on the highway."

"Traffic started moving right after I texted," Mike said. The weariness showed on his face. "I wanted to see you, though. Any chance we could meet for breakfast tomorrow? The Cayman trip spoiled me – I miss seeing you every day."

They settled in on the couch as Kristen replied. "I can't do breakfast," she said. "I've got a client in crisis. I'm seeing her at nine. She and her fiancé had a big fight."

"Crisis? Fight? Kristen, this is what I hate about your work. What if he shows up full of anger? How can I know you'll be safe?"

Kristen looked at Mike, her eyes wide and breathing labored. "It will be fine. The building will be full of people at nine in the morning. Mike, what's really going on? I thought we had this all settled. My work is important to me."

"We're about to be married, Kristen," Mike said, rubbing his tired eyes. "I can't let anything happen to you. Sophie and I need you."

His simple plea touched Kristen, but she didn't know how to break through his deluded belief that he could keep her safe from any and all threats. Life was too random for that. Why couldn't he understand?

Steadying herself, she did her best to avoid a fight. Their time in Grand Cayman had been so wonderful. Why did Mike have to get protective and possessive now? Something was up.

"Honey, I'm trying to understand," she said. "I know you and Sophie need me. I need you, too. But life is unpredictable. It's folly to think we can control everything that happens to us. Thousands of mental health professionals work each day unharmed. What else is going on with you?"

"Nothing," Mike said flatly. "I need to go. We'll talk tomorrow evening."

With that, he was gone. Bernie whimpered, not having received his usual belly rub from Mike. "I know, pal," Kristen said as she hugged Bernie. "Mike's not himself. I wonder what happened when he dropped Sophie off at Anita's?"

Chapter Fourteen

Mike entered his home completely spent after the day of driving Sophie to Indy, driving back in jammed highway traffic, and then arguing with Kristen about the safety of her job. How was he going to handle his fears? Kristen was right – there was no way he could keep her, or anyone else for that matter, safe from the perils of this imperfect world.

He had allowed Anita's attitude to trigger his negative outlook. After their improved interactions of late, Mike had hoped she would congratulate him on his engagement. Sophie spilled the beans, of course, shouting as she came through Anita's door, "Kristen and Daddy are getting married! He got her a big ring from a snooty English guy."

Anita had looked shocked, then hurt. What could she be bothered about? She'd practically given Mike her blessing to marry Kristen. He'd have to quit trying to predict her moods.

"Wow, that's great news," Anita said. "A big ring, huh? That's better than I got from Daddy."

Mike had steeled himself, refusing to let Anita play the martyr, something he thought she'd gotten over with her new marriage to Grant. "I thought you loved my mother's ring," he said softly. "You still have it. You can have the stone reset into a necklace if you want. Or you can save it for Sophie."

"Sure. I'm very happy for you and Kristen," Anita said, her flat look indicating an obvious lack of happiness. Grant came in and volunteered to help Sophie unpack her suitcase, allowing the conversation between Mike and Anita to continue uninterrupted.

"What is it really? I thought you liked Kristen."

"I do. I'm happy for you both," Anita repeated. "I guess Sophie's enthusiasm reminded me we never did the ring shopping thing, or pondered what style to get, or how much to spend."

"My mother's ring is worth far more than the ring I bought Kristen." Mike had paused, ready to question Anita's priorities, especially since she'd been so petty in front of Sophie. He wasn't into fighting, though. "But you're right – we didn't have the shopping experience most couples have. I'm sorry about that."

Anita had seemed appeased. "It's no biggie. I'm not at my best tonight. Stomach bug, I'm guessing. Drive carefully on your way back to Gordon, Mike." And he had been sent on his way.

Staring at his mostly empty refrigerator, Mike's mood continued to sour. He needed to eat, but a cold sandwich had no appeal. The two women in his life were stressing him. His clinical acumen knew he was allowing them to dull his appetite, but he decided to go with his morose frame of mind.

No matter what he did, someone was unhappy. Kristen didn't feel cherished by his concerns about her clients; she felt smothered. Anita wasn't happy Sophie would have a good woman as a stepmom; she was jealous of Mike's fresh start, easily forgetting she and Grant had made a new start for themselves.

What's really important? Mike asked himself. *I love Kristen, and if I don't trust her judgment, I'll lose her.*

Too tired to talk, he texted his fiancée. "I'm sorry, sweetie. I'm tired and cranky. I know you're a great psychologist, one who will help your client tomorrow like no one else can."

He waited for nearly ten minutes, wondering if Kristen was ignoring him. She finally replied. "You're forgiven. I love you." The heart emoji also helped soothe Mike's mood.

Heather arrived fifteen minutes early for her session. She was fresh-faced but looked tired. Kristen avoided questions, letting her tell the story of the fight with Cody.

"We were having a good time looking at menus from the wedding caterer," Heather began. "But when I pointed out chicken would be less expensive than mini-filets, he blew up. He accused me of running the whole show and not letting him have any input about the wedding. He said he couldn't even choose his tux – my mom suggested this sharp design at a place where she can get a discount." Heather stopped and became tearful. "Then he left, slamming the door on his way out. And I called you."

"Have you heard from him?" Kristen asked.

"Yes, he texted he was staying in a friend's basement. He's working all day today. I hope he'll be back for supper." Wringing her hands, Heather continued. "What if I've failed at having a relationship, too? I ruined my chances for grad school, my body is changing in ways you can't imagine, I got you fired, and I'll have a baby to raise on my own. Life as I know it is over."

Kristen decided a little tough love was what Heather needed. "Heather, stop. Do you see how you're spiraling down? You've turned an argument, one that will heal itself with a little love and humility, into a pending break-up and total life failure."

"You think?"

"I know. You and Cody are under tremendous pressure, but despite it all you've both stepped up and made what you believe to be the best decision for yourselves and your baby. You told me yourself you'd get to grad school eventually. I told you life experience would help you grow into an excellent therapist. This is some of the life experience I was talking about. Also, I've gotten my tenure-track job back, beginning in the spring. The provost called me yesterday. So that concern is off your plate."

"Really? How did that happen? When I saw the provost, he just listened to me. He didn't add two words, and then his admin came in and announced the appointment was over."

"I'm not sure what changed his mind, but I'm grateful," Kristen said with a smile. "Your visit to the provost certainly helped."

"Great, Dr. Anderson. But back to me. How do I convince Cody he's part of the wedding?"

Kristen smiled inwardly at Heather's self-absorption. The young woman was maturing, but in fits and starts.

"By letting him *be* part of the wedding. I'm not trying to be mean, but how much have you and your mom let Cody do? Is it really his wedding or just yours?"

Heather sat still. Her face clouded with uncertainty, anger, and finally awareness. "You're making a good point. I assumed guys didn't care about wedding details. I took over, and what I couldn't do I let my mom cover."

"Assuming we know what our partners are thinking is usually a bad idea," Kristen said, remembering Mike's mood last night. "You've got to talk to Cody the way you're talking to me. Ask him directly what he wants his wedding to be like. Isn't it odd how you've used sexist assumptions on the man you love?"

"What sexist assumptions? I'm a feminist, Dr. Anderson. You know that."

"But wouldn't a feminist believe a groom should be an integral part of his wedding?"

Heather pondered this. "Maybe. Well, yes. I get it, Dr. Anderson. Thanks for seeing me on such short notice. I've got to call Cody. And by the way, you're invited to the wedding."

Kristen sighed. *If only all my crisis clients were this easy. Those two have some quick growing up to do, but they'll be okay.*

Mike spent the day unpacking, doing laundry, and replenishing his pantry and fridge. Worried about Kristen and her client in crisis, he called her as soon as he thought her day would be over. She answered on the first ring.

"Hey," Kristen said softly. "How are you today?"

"Better. I was exhausted and irritated. You got the brunt of it, and I'm sorry."

Kristen knew exhaustion was only part of the story. "Other

than traffic and being tired, what's got you on edge? Did Anita say something about us?"

"As always, you're right on target. She was miffed because she and I didn't shop for rings. She got my mother's ring but believe me, she wasn't shortchanged. It's a beautiful ring with a vintage setting."

"There's probably more to it than that," Kristen noted. "I feel for you, though. You'd had a long day and had to say goodbye to Sophie after our wonderful week together."

"Yes, that's it. Anita and I have come a long way, but I realize there's still a lot of hurt and anger in both of us. Luckily Grant took Sophie to another room while we talked."

"Did you have a big argument?"

"No, believe it or not, I kept my cool. She seemed to appreciate my understanding of her resentment of Mom's ring."

"We'll see. My sense is we'll figure this out soon. And maybe it's not a bad thing – the better we all communicate the easier our lives will be."

Mike was astounded at Kristen's charitable attitude toward Anita. "I love you. So much. It seems like longer than two days since we've had any time together."

"I agree. You were in such a mood after your trip to Indy, I didn't tell you my big news. I'm on tenure-track again as of spring semester. Evidently the dean has been a problem for a while now."

"That's great!" Mike yelled into the phone. "No one deserves it more. We should celebrate."

"I'm saving my pennies for the wedding. You should be saving for a honeymoon. The Cayman trip was great, but I want to experience a beach trip without Sophie. I love her, of course, but we need to be alone."

"Amen to that," Mike said fervently. "Saving our money doesn't preclude a celebration dinner, though. Where would you like to go this weekend?"

"Now you're sounding like Dr. Moneybags, which is what Annie calls you," Kristen said with a laugh. "Don't tell her I said that."

"Don't worry, I won't. My question stands. Where should we celebrate?"

"Somewhere local. I've only got a few weeks before the Fall Fest, so I can't devote an entire evening to our fun. How about the place you took me with all the comfort food?"

"Good idea. I'll see you on Friday."

Mike and Kristen ended the call, with Mike sighing with relief at her forgiveness and her reinstatement at GCC. With some guilt, he admitted to himself he was grateful Kristen's full-time teaching load would prevent her from taking on more clients in her private practice. But he still worried about her and probably always would.

He needed to monitor his protective nature. Kristen was very sensitive to his concerns about her clientele. She constantly reminded him most violent crimes were not committed by those with mental illness. She repeatedly told him about her careful referral process, and how she and Lauren had each other's back. He just wished he could believe it.

His phone jingled, and he wondered what Kristen had forgotten to say. The ID named Anita, however. *Great,* he thought. *More grief headed my way.*

"Anything wrong?" he asked Anita. "Did Sophie have a bad night?"

"Nothing's wrong. I need to give you my apologies. Grant reamed me out after you left. He was right – I was snippy and childish about your engagement."

"We're all breaking new ground. And Sophie sprung it on you in the most sudden way possible."

"The 'new ground' has more to it than you know. The stomach bug I mentioned is actually morning sickness. Or all-day sickness, in my case. Sophie's going to have lots of adjusting to do."

"That's spectacular news! But I thought you and Grant liked the quiet life. What changed?"

"He loves Sophie so much he wanted a child of his own before it was too late," Anita replied. "I agreed – our marriage is a good one, and a child will be a welcome addition."

"So, does Sophie know? Have you and Grant told her she's going to be a big sister?"

"We told her last night after you left. She was worried because I spent most of the evening in the bathroom throwing up. She's over the moon. I think she's excited to have someone to boss around!"

"Anita, I'm so happy for you and Grant. I mean that with all my heart. You'll be a great team with your little one, and with his or her big sister. Tell Grant for me, okay?"

"It's a boy," Anita said with pride. "The sonogram revealed that while you were in Grand Cayman. Anyway, my attitude last night was unforgivable. I'm sorry. Tell Kristen I'm happy for you both."

The call ended with good feelings on both sides. Maybe he and Anita were finally bridging the gap between being estranged x-spouses and friendly co-parents. Mike couldn't wait to tell Kristen about the baby, but he wanted to do it in person. The news would have to wait until Friday.

Kristen was thrilled when Mike shared Anita's news. "I told you it was something that could be good. Sophie will have a brother! What a joy. You know what else? She'll be even happier to stay with us, because she won't have to share attention with a baby."

"That's sounds uncharacteristically selfish," Mike teased. "I think Sophie likes being with us whether or not there's a baby to compete with."

They arrived at Kristen's after their carb-laden dinners. She showed Mike her inventory for the Fall Fest. "Do you think it's enough? Ten days is a long time to be open for business."

Kristen's dining room looked like the home décor section of a department store. Mike studied the huge pile of crafts. They ranged from large wreaths to tiny tree ornaments. Kristen had added some pieces of jewelry, made with bits of fabric and leather. There were nursery items for both genders and oven mitts decorated with holiday trim. She'd even made some collars for dogs of all sizes. Mike knew she was ready for the Fest.

"I think you'll be fine, honey," he said. "As you asked me recently, what else is going on? You've got enough inventory to stock a major online retailer. What are you afraid of?"

Kristen studied him. "Good catch. I'm just anxious about a few things. Actually, many things. I have three jobs, a fiancé, a step-daughter-to-be, a widowed mother, and a wedding to plan. My life is chaos."

"Or are you scared of being married to me? And all that entails?" Mike hesitated, knowing his question was a loaded one. Between his temper, new job, Sophie, and the Anita/Grant/baby trio, Kristen was taking on a lot. He held his breath, desperately wanting her to say she had no doubts at all.

"You're good. That's it exactly. I think in bed each night about what my new life will be like, and I can't quite envision it. My current chaos is at least familiar. What if we fight? What if I'm late one evening with a client and you call 911? What if you decide you don't like your new job, and you want to move back to Indianapolis? What if Anita doesn't like my parenting style?"

"Those are all excellent questions, honey. The theme sounds familiar, though. Didn't I get a lecture from you recently about not being able to control the randomness of life? Didn't you say life is unpredictable?"

Kristen nodded, and Mike continued. "Well, then, it seems I'm not the only one with control issues." He laughed and reached for Kristen, kissing her soundly. He wrapped her in his arms and led her to the sofa. Leaning against him, she kissed him back, even more soundly.

"I do NOT have control issues," Kristen protested. Her laugh gave her away, however. "You're right, Mike. We're a real pair. How will we handle things when we butt heads?"

"Like this," he murmured. He kissed Kristen, long, hard, and filled with need. "We'll kiss and makeup as often as we need to. Probably even when we don't need to!"

Fall Fest arrived, and therefore Kristen's chaotic life kicked into high gear. She drafted friends to help staff her booth while she was teaching or seeing clients. Mike stopped by when he had the time to drive to Parke County, but training for his new role at work kept him busy most days.

On the first Saturday of the Fest Mike was able to get away from the hospital. Parking was tight, and he walked several minutes to reach the barn housing the craft booths. He spotted Kristen before she saw him.

Look at her, he thought. *She loves people. They buy her crafts, then linger and talk for several minutes while she helps other customers. It's foolish for me to think I can stop her from counseling, teaching, or whatever she wants to do. It's all in her DNA. She's a natural people person. Without all this, she'd be lost.*

Kristen glanced at the tree where Mike was hiding. "Hey, are you stalking me?" she asked.

"Not funny," he said with a fake pout. "You know I worry about that sort of thing. I was admiring you, actually. You're having the time of your life here. I'm almost feeling left out."

"Quit it. You're having fun, too. I bet you're calculating how much extra we'll have to spend on the honeymoon. Seriously, I'm going to run out of stock, which was my worst fear."

"It will be okay, though," she continued, trying to convince herself. "I talked to the sales manager, and he's got a vendor who didn't make the registration deadline willing to cover my space. I may be out of here a few days early."

"That's okay," Mike said. "You look tired – happy, but tired."

"True. I am tired. It's been a good day, but stressful, too. Lauren stopped by with her baby. My surprise best sellers have been items for a baby's nursery. It feels like I'm the only one without a baby in my life." Kristen looked away. "Even Anita and Grant are expecting."

"My love, we can take care of that. Are you saying you want a family soon? I'll do everything in my power to help." Mike grinned as he looked at Kristen with a sexy side eye.

"We'll see. First, I need to get through the wedding and then recover on my beach honeymoon. If you're a dutiful husband, we'll discuss having babies."

"No worries there," Mike teased back. "My picture will be in the dictionary under 'dutiful husband.'"

The month leading up to the ceremony was hectic but full of joy. Kristen worked frantically as she designed the perfect wedding. *Perfect, but within my budget,* she thought. *Mom's offer of money was sweet, but she needs every dime she has. She's going to live a long, fulfilling life. She should be able to enjoy it.*

Taking a break from classes and clients, Kristen visited Lauren three weeks before the wedding. "Baby Thomas is a doll," Kristen gushed. "He's pretty robust for a preemie. What's in your breast milk?"

Lauren smiled back as she burped her son. "Nothing special, just lots of love," she answered. "Thanks for the gifts for the baby's room. They're all the more special because you made them yourself. Of course, the gift from Grand Cayman also has special meaning," Lauren teased. "While you were in the most romantic place on earth, you thought of my baby."

"You're very welcome," Kristen said, ignoring Lauren's humor. "The craft gifts also fit my budget perfectly, since I'm planning a frugal wedding. My last and most difficult challenge is the dress."

"The dress! Kristen, you've only got a few weeks – what do you plan to wear?" Lauren's outburst startled little Thomas, so she quickly smothered him with kisses while she rocked him in her arms.

"My absolute fallback plan is a dress I got off the rack on a prom display. It's a Grecian look – lots of draped off-white fabric and simple lines."

"It's doesn't exactly scream 'here comes the bride,' does it?" Lauren asked. "Your face gives you away, Kristen. Any other options?"

"Mom's offered her dress, which would have been okay, but it has a yellow stain center front. The dry cleaner said there's no way to fix it after thirty-five years. I tried to find lace to cover it, but nothing matches. The Grecian dress will be fine. The important thing is Mike and I will be married."

Thomas whimpered as he tried to place his thumb in his mouth. "This baby is ready for his nap," Lauren said. "I'll be right back."

Lauren returned a few minutes later with her own wedding dress on a hanger. "What about my dress?" she asked Kristen. "You're five inches taller than I am, but we could cut it down to tea length. The designer in me has a few ideas about changes that would make the dress your own."

"What? You'd be willing to destroy your dress for me?" Kristen's eyes filled as she absorbed the generous love of her friend.

"I've got loads of pictures and videos of this dress. You've saved my maternity leave by seeing most of my clients, even Heather, for which I'm eternally grateful. I heard through the grapevine, meaning your friend Annie, about your dress dilemma. Bryan and I discussed this, and he's fine with me giving you my gown."

Tears spilled as Kristen hugged her friend. "I'd be honored, Lauren. But the top still has to fit me, right?"

"That would be the ideal scenario," Lauren said, as she studied the dress. "You're tall, but small-boned like me. Take it to the spare bedroom and give it a try."

Kristen returned wearing the dress, which did fit her well in the bodice. The length hit at an awkward spot, though, just above her ankles. "It's gorgeous," Kristen breathed. "I'd wear it as is."

"No, we can do better. My designer juices have been flowing ever since I talked to Annie. Here are my ideas – Ombre tulle layers under the top white tulle layer, in a pastel color of your choosing. Draped cap sleeves off each shoulder, with beading to match the beads I'll sew to the bodice front. And I'd shorten the length about six inches to make a classic tea-length skirt."

Kristen was thrilled, but her crafting skills were limited to glue guns and straight stitching on placemats. "What's an Ombre skirt? I think I know what draped cap sleeves are. And are you sure about cutting that much length off?"

"Ombre is very trendy. It's a graduated look of color, nothing severe. You start light and go darker, or vice versa. And the length will be perfect a few inches shorter. I may add lace edging to give it a more formal look."

"I still don't get the Ombre thing. Really, the dress is fine."

"What's your favorite wedding color?" Lauren asked, ignoring Kristen's confusion.

"I don't have one. But pink is Sophie's 'Number One,' so she'd be thrilled if I had pink in my dress."

"Perfect. Imagine a light pink tulle underlayer, then a darker layer under that, finishing off with a deeper pink, almost crimson, layer toward the bottom of the skirt. I'll drape the layers, so they won't look choppy. And we could replace my sash with a pink jeweled sash to coordinate the whole look." Lauren leaned back, proud of her inspiration.

"It does sound perfect. But even if we start with your dress, I can't let you pay for all that. It's got to be expensive. And I'll need a veil, too. I wasn't going to worry about a headpiece with the Grecian-look dress, but yours is too fancy not to have a veil."

"Tulle for the Ombre look is cheap. My veil can be your 'something borrowed.' And I've already researched sashes on Etsy. They're very affordable compared to those in bridal shops."

"Okay, I'm convinced," Kristen said, again tearing up. "But what about the timing? You're a new mom with a baby to tend to. How will you be able to do all this?"

"Already covered," Lauren said with a smug grin. "Thomas's two grandmas have signed up for shifts to watch him. Even though it all sounds complex, I'll have your dress done in a few days."

Lauren did some preliminary measuring and instructed Kristen to return the next evening for a fitting. Kristen was still concerned.

"Are you absolutely sure?" she asked Lauren. "One-hundred percent? This is your wedding dress, after all."

"Two-hundred percent," Lauren said with conviction. "You'll pay it forward – I know you. This is what life is about. Friends, family, giving to others. So, no more doubts. Your dress will be splendid."

Mike came over for supper that night after a long day at work. "I love the hours," he complained, "but the personnel stuff is ornery. One doctor said I had no right to challenge his chart notes. They consist of a maximum of five words, like 'Patient doing better.' No discussion of labs, tests, or the patient's complaints. It's a lawsuit waiting to happen."

"Are you sorry you took the job?" Kristen asked. "If you want to look elsewhere, or go back to your original schedule, we'll make it work."

"Thanks for that. I'm just venting. I sort of enjoy using my new skills. I'm learning to be confrontational without becoming angry. And since I still get to see patients, it's the perfect mix."

"But what about you?" he continued. "You were going to Cincinnati with Annie to look for a dress. Any luck?"

"No need for a road trip. I stopped by Lauren's to give her the gifts I'd made for the baby. Annie told her about my dress dilemma, and Lauren offered to remake her dress for me. I think she's enjoying it, but I still feel a little guilty."

"One thing we know about Lauren is she's a determined person," Mike said. "If she offered, she's sure. But are you okay with wearing someone else's dress? Do we need to delay the wedding?"

"No, I'm honored by her gift. Based on what she described, it will be an entirely different look from her original design."

"I'm relieved to hear we can get married on schedule," Mike said with a dramatic sigh. "This wedding can't happen soon enough for me."

Epilogue

Despite the late date in November, the Gordon Community College commons had several trees still sporting orange and rust-colored leaves. Annie and Katie had fashioned a canopy decorated with artificial greenery and sprays of mums. Gourds and pumpkins were arranged in a path leading to the chairs lined in rows for guests. A heated tent was in place a few yards away, where guests would lunch on country-baked ham, sweet potato casserole, and layered salad. Kaye had outdone herself with the three-tiered cake, thankful she could contribute to the wedding after all.

Kristen dressed inside the student union building, empty of students due to the Thanksgiving holiday break. Annie, Katie, Kaye, and Sophie drew a collective gasp when Kristen appeared in her dress. Lauren stood to one side, grinning proudly at her creation.

"Pink is my 'Number One' and your dress has lots of it!" Sophie cheered. "It almost matches my dress."

"That Ombre look is stunning," Annie said. "Vera Wang has been doing that. It's so on trend."

"Am I the only one who's never heard of Ombre?" Kristen asked, shaking her head as she attached her veil to her curly hair. "It's a good thing I have a friend who's a fashionista. I'd be wearing that prom dress without Lauren's help."

"You look lovely, honey," Kaye said as her eyes misted. "Your dad would have been very proud. I know he's here, though. Fall was his favorite time of year. Remember how he'd decorate in October with more flair than at Christmas?"

Kristen, Katie, and Kaye hugged as they thought of their missing husband and father. "No time for tears, though," Kaye said breaking away. "We have a wedding to get to."

Reverend Taylor's remarks were perfectly suited to the newly married couple. He highlighted their personality strengths, their differences, and the need for God's presence in every marriage. He made an inside joke about discovering new faith while dealing with the perfection of the Proverbs woman, at which Kristen and Mike dissolved in quiet laughter. His reference to the Psalms, "Be still, and know that I am God," resonated strongly with the happy pair. Kristen then kissed her groom, grateful that she now understood more about God's blessings.

As she and Mike walked to the tent, she asked, "What's with this wedding ring, dear husband? I thought we were going with simple gold bands. My engagement ring is beautiful. You didn't have to get me a yellow diamond band to match."

"There are times, dear wife, that your frugality is frustrating. I wanted your wedding band to reflect how much I love you, and how much I've changed since we've been together."

Kissing her husband tenderly, Kristen replied, "I've changed, too. You make me a better person. I'm still an optimist, but I also know God is with us no matter what life brings."

They both looked around as they heard Sophie's distinctive high-pitched voice. Decked out in her hot pink dress, she announced to the wedding crowd, "I have two *familigias* now! It's a good thing I think before I speak!"

Discussion Questions

1. At the start of the book, Kristen tried to be optimistic. She believed in karma but had trouble believing in God's love after her father's death. What would you say to her about God's role in our lives?
2. Mike's temper was evident at the beginning of the story. What feelings were masked by his anger? How did Kristen help him understand himself better?
3. Mike's need to avoid another marital mistake resulted in his search for the perfect Proverbs woman. What do Kristen's and Anita's reactions to this quest say about Mike? About themselves?
4. Grief is a major theme in *Crafted with Love*. In what areas are Kristen, Mike, Sophie, Anita, and Kaye grieving? How do they work through their pain?
5. Heather's tirade to the dean causes more chaos in Kristen's life. How did Kristen handle her new situation? Could you have forgiven Heather?
6. Kaye's depression is partially due to health issues. What do you think about the mind/body connection?
7. To what factors would you attribute Sophie's growth spurt?

Coming Soon!

Annie's story will be the third and final book in the Indiana Romance Series. Find out how the sassy nurse practioner manages to fill in for a colleague at the campus health office while dealing with a new college administrator intent on saving money. As you would expect, Annie's brand of humor and teasing promises a novel with lots of charm and romance. Dr. Ben Upton had better have his best administrative skills ready as he copes with Annie's sincere, and constant, challenges!

Enjoy this sample from ***Prescription for TLC:***

Annie stayed at the wedding reception for just barely the appropriate amount of time, and then she began to make her way to the exit of the heated tent. Kristen looked angelic, Mike was full of joy, and little Sophie enjoyed using the few Italian words she knew. To everyone's delight, she repeatedly emphasized she had two *famiglias* now.

"Hey, lady, are you leaving?" Kristen asked, rushing to meet Annie by the draped opening. "The party's just begun. And since you've known Mike longer than I have, you need to stick around in case there's any relationship repairing to be done. Weddings are very stressful for the new couple, you know."

Annie appreciated Kristen's attempt and knew the bride should have been talking to her other guests. "No, Mrs. Sutliff, you and Mike are well on your way to wedded bliss. It's obvious to all. Really, though, I need to scoot. My pager coverage ends at five, and then, despite his insistence that he's the consummate professional, my slacker colleague will refuse to answer his pager or phone. Medical emergencies wait for no one. I'll sure be glad when covering for Campus Health ends."

Kristen eyed her friend closely. "I know what you're doing, Annie. You're making a quick escape. You'll be in a wedding gown soon, mark my words. But get going, if you must. I'll call you when we get back from the Bahamas."

The two friends hugged, and Annie made her way to the parking lot of the Gordon Community College commons. She thought she'd made a clean getaway when another voice called her name.

"Annie, wait up," Reverend Taylor said. "I'm on my way out, too. Great wedding, if I do say so myself."

Tilting her head and smiling at Josh Taylor, Annie stopped her hasty retreat. "Doesn't pride go before a fall, Reverend? You did a fine job with the ceremony, but you seem to be looking for compliments."

"Yes, I am," he replied. "Quit with the Reverend stuff. We've only known each other since first grade. It's always been Josh. Anyway, why aren't you staying for the rest of the evening? Kristen's one of your best friends."

"Duty calls. My pager will blow up soon."

Josh rolled his eyes. "Annie, I've seen you take an active pager to concerts, parties of every sort, and on trips with your girlfriend posse. You've answered pages with ease by finding an empty room and using your laptop apps to check medications and treatment plans. You're the ideal nurse practitioner who still manages to have a personal life. Why are you really leaving?"

"I'm tired, out of sorts, and this bridesmaid's dress only fits due to the tightest undergarment known to man. Mom used to have a girdle, but today's modern woman uses a specially engineered tortuous bodysuit. My Italian form needs to breathe."

"Lame, Annie," Josh said calmly. "Let's go get a latte, and you can tell me what's bothering you. Without all the underwear details, of course."

CPSIA information can be obtained
at www.ICGtesting.com
Printed in the USA
BVHW031936100320
574644BV00001B/9